"I was waiting for you."

Savannah's relief at having someone finally answer the door was stifled by Blake's words. All in black, illuminated only by a flickering candle he held, he didn't look like a safe retreat from the storm.

Blake was looking at her closely. Too closely. Savannah resisted the impulse to cover her scarred cheek with her palm. "You might have had a long wait."

"No," he said. "I knew you'd come."

"I'm not accustomed to auditioning."

He nodded. "I thought it was important that I see how we work together. I'll show you to your room."

Unwilling to let the faint candle flare out of her sight, Savannah followed close on his heels. Something brushed against her legs. Relief rushed over her when she viewed the midnight-black cat at her feet. Blake would have a black familiar. "Am I here so that you can see if we're compatible?"

Blake stopped and assessed her from head to foot. "Not exactly. You're here so that I can discover whether or not I can work with you without taking you to bed."

JoAnn Ross and the Temptation editors were walking along the Toronto waterfront when vampires naturally came up in the conversation. We all agreed that vampires were very romantic— unrequited love, danger, etc. As well, JoAnn told us about an idea she'd had kicking around for some time, the story of two people badly hurt by love who meet at an enchanted isolated house. Imagine our delight a few months later, when the combination of these two ideas arrived as *Dark Desires*!

As this is the month that honors lovers, Harlequin is celebrating with MY VALENTINE 1992. JoAnn's *A Very Special Delivery* is one of the wonderful short stories that focus on Valentine's Day. The collection includes other stories by popular Temptation authors Gina Wilkins, Kristine Rolofson and Vicki Lewis Thompson.

In September 1992, *The Knight in Shining Armor* by JoAnn Ross will be a part of Rebels & Rogues—our yearlong salute to Temptation heroes. Don't miss this story about a hero who cares too much.

Dark Desires

JoAnn Ross

Harlequin Books

TORONTO • NEW YORK • LONDON
AMSTERDAM • PARIS • SYDNEY • HAMBURG
STOCKHOLM • ATHENS • TOKYO • MILAN
MADRID • WARSAW • BUDAPEST • AUCKLAND

To my editor, Malle Vallik, who understands the fantasy

Published February 1992

ISBN 0-373-25482-2

DARK DESIRES

1

"I'VE GOT a proposal for you."

Savannah Starr crossed her long legs, sat back in the white wrought-iron chair and eyed the man seated across the umbrella-topped table with suspicion. Justin Peters had been pitching the same offer for the past three weeks. She'd been tossing it back into his lap for the identical length of time.

"If it's what I think it is," she said, "the answer's still no." Flashing him a sweet but firm smile, she began searching through her seafood salad for elusive bay shrimp.

Normally known for his unflappability, Justin Peters allowed his frustration to surface. "Anyone ever tell you that you take after your old man?"

Savannah's father was a phenomenon in the music business: a British-born rock singer whose glittering star continued to rise after thirty years in the business. Over those years, Reggie Starr had been described as cheeky, unbelievably sexy, irreverent, irresistible, and brilliant. He was also infamous for his insistence on doing things his own way.

"Since it isn't considered good form for an agent to insult a client, I'll assume you meant that as a compliment," Savannah said calmly.

Justin Peters's answering expression was one of ex-
asperation mixed with affection. He'd known Savannah for all of her twenty-six years. As agent to not only
Savannah, but her father and equally famous mother,
actress/sex-symbol Melanie Raine, he'd been on the
scene at Savannah's birth, had comforted her when her
parents divorced the summer of her seventh year and
had been the only member of her "family" who'd managed to show up for her high-school graduation.

Eighteen months ago, he'd grieved with her over her
mother's death; six months later, he'd rushed to her
hospital bed, where, ignoring threats from her doctors
and seething glares from her nurses, he'd remained for
three days until she'd been declared out of danger.

Although he'd been married five times, none of those
marriages had resulted in children. Now, at sixty-five,
Justin had no intention of marrying again. Which made
Savannah the closest thing to a daughter he'd ever have.
Which was fine with him. Because he couldn't love her
more if she were his own flesh and blood.

"I still think you're making a mistake," he said,
swirling his drink. "The role of Scarlett O'Hara only
comes around every fifty years or so."

There had been a time when Savannah would have
lusted for a chance to play the world-famous vixen in
the long-awaited sequel to *Gone with the Wind.* But for
someone who'd grown up in a town where dreams and
reality often became distorted, she was incredibly well-
grounded. She'd also been born with a deep-seated
sense of honesty that made it impossible for her to lie.
Even to herself—*especially* to herself.

With a sigh, she put her fork down and met his frustrated gaze with a resigned one of her own. "I appreciate the vote of confidence, Justin," she said gently. "And twelve months ago, I would have jumped at the chance. But a lot has changed." Her fingers unconsciously brushed against her cheek, drawing his attention to the faint line that went from her ear to the corner of her lips. The scar was one of several bearing mute evidence to last year's horror.

"If you're worried about your scars, they're barely visible," he insisted, not for the first time.

"They've faded a lot," Savannah agreed. "Especially since the dermabrasion. But closeup lenses are brutal."

"All the years in the business and you haven't heard of soft-focus lenses?"

His teasing question earned a faint smile. "Forget the Vaseline or cheesecloth, they'd have to shoot me through denim."

Justin frowned. "Savannah, you're okay with all this, aren't you?"

Try as he might, he couldn't forget the pain her mother had experienced when forced to face the fact that she was no longer the sexy young bombshell who'd been discovered selling stockings at Saks. When her stunning beauty began to fade, rather than have her legion of fans watch her age, Melanie Raine had committed suicide. Her untimely death had made headlines around the world; thousands of her distraught fans had descended on Forest Lawn for a lavish funeral befitting the woman who'd been described as the Goddess of Lust.

The fleeting pain in Savannah's dark eyes revealed that she, too, was thinking of her mother—the very same woman who had once told her adoring five-year-old daughter that without beauty, a woman was nothing.

"Emotionally, I'm fine. Physically..." She shrugged. "Let's just say that it's been a rough year. I'm glad it's over. And I'm eager to get back to work."

"But not in front of the camera."

"No." Her soft tone was firm. Final. "I enjoyed acting, but that part of my life is over. I've spent the past twenty years of my life utilizing talents I inherited from my mother. From now on, I'm concentrating on my father's branch of my genetic tree."

"Speaking of music," Justin said with forced casualness, "I had dinner Saturday night with a client who admired your score for *Seduced*."

The movie about a Southern siren who seduced a married police detective in order to convince him to kill her rich elderly husband had been Savannah's last role, and although she suspected that her Best Actress Oscar, awarded while she was still in the hospital, had been influenced by a strong sympathy vote, she was nevertheless proud of her work.

But as much as she appreciated receiving the highest accolade that could have been granted her by her acting peers, she was exceptionally pleased with the way the movie's sound track—the first she'd ever done—had gained her immediate recognition in the music community—a recognition that didn't appear to have been influenced by her father's fame.

"Oh?" she asked idly, beginning to relax, now that she had determined that Justin wasn't going to argue for her returning to the screen anymore. "Anyone I know?" She took a sip of white wine.

"Blake Winters."

"Ah." Savannah nodded. "The wunderkind."

Although she'd never met the reclusive screen-writer/director/producer, his reputation as a maverick stood out in a herd-mentality town like Hollywood. There were other rumors, as well, Savannah remembered—especially about an accident concerning his former wife. But she'd been in the hospital at the time and didn't know the details.

"Since I've heard he's quite difficult to please, I suppose I should be flattered," she said.

"Blake's a perfectionist," Justin agreed. "But he knows talent when he sees it. Or in this case, hears it." He leaned back, glass in hand, and sipped his Scotch. "He's just finished his latest picture."

"I read something about it last week in *Variety*," she recalled. "Is it true that the cast and crew had to swear not to divulge the plot or risk never working for him again?"

"No one was actually forced to agree to those terms," Justin corrected.

"But they all agreed?"

"Blake is particularly close to this story. He doesn't want it hashed over in the press before he can get it to the screen."

"Well, he sounds paranoid to me," Savannah decided. She speared an artichoke heart and popped it into her mouth.

"Isn't everyone, in this town?"

"I suppose so. But from what I've heard, if you look up the word *paranoia* in the dictionary, you'll find Blake Winters's picture. I also read that whenever he shot on location, he made the crew wear T-shirts suggesting they were working on a sci-fi film, instead of a black comedy about his marriage... That *is* what the film's about? His marriage?"

"All Blake's movies are somewhat autobiographical," Justin hedged. "As for the T-shirts—I thought that was a particularly brilliant stroke of genius."

"Or dementia," she countered. "Anyone that distrustful should be weaving baskets in some quiet sanitarium or, at the very least, making spy films."

Taking another sip of the crisp, dry, house wine, she made a mental note to ask the waiter the label. It would be nice to serve at parties. Not that she'd done much entertaining in the past year. Actually, Savannah admitted to herself, she hadn't done any entertaining in the past twelve months. Perhaps Justin had been right, last week, when he'd accused her of becoming a hermit.

"The Cold War's over," Justin pointed out, breaking into her introspection. "Which effectively rules out spy stories. And if Blake is a little wary of people—and I'm not agreeing that he is—did you ever consider that he might have a reason to be?"

"Ouch." Savannah grimaced. "I think I've just been put in my place. Live and let live—is that what you're saying?"

"I was merely suggesting that you withhold judgment until you meet the guy."

Savannah eyed him over the rim of her wineglass. "This proposal you asked me to lunch to discuss," she said slowly, "would it have anything to do with Blake Winters's new film?"

"He wants you to audition to lay the track," Justin divulged, looking immensely pleased with himself.

Two thoughts flew through Savannah's mind, the first being that she was being offered a chance to work with one of Hollywood's premiere talents. The second was that the man actually expected her to *audition*.

"I haven't tried out for a part since I was fourteen years old," she reminded Justin unnecessarily.

"By that time you'd already been in the business for eight years," he countered. "Everyone knew what you could do in front of the camera. But working in a studio, fitting music to moving pictures, is a whole different ball of wax, sweetheart."

"You've already said he liked the sound track for *Seduced*. Surely that work speaks for itself."

"It might—with any other director," Justin agreed. "But Blake's got his own way of working, Savannah. And he needs to feel that all the creative people on his team fully understand and appreciate what he's trying to do."

"Audition." Savannah put down her glass and dragged her hand through her thick, shoulder-length black hair. "The idea of writing a song on spec, so some arrogant paranoid can determine whether or not I can understand his artistic intent, is ridiculous."

She frowned and directed her attention toward the steady stream of traffic making its way up Sunset

Boulevard. "What's even worse is that I'm actually considering doing it."

"It'd be good for you to get back to work again," Justin pointed out, telling Savannah nothing that she hadn't been telling herself for weeks. "And since you categorically refuse to work in front of the camera, I'd say this is a golden opportunity." Point made, he returned his attention to his lunch, cutting into his prime-rib sandwich with gusto.

He was right. Although Blake Winters wasn't the most prolific individual in town—his last film, a starring vehicle for his former wife, had been released three years ago—he was one of the most talented—perhaps even the very best in the business. The chance to work with him was enough of a lure that Savannah was willing to put aside her own pride. For now.

"All right, I'll do it," she decided. "So, when can you get me a rough cut?"

"I'm afraid it's not that simple."

Of course not. From what little she'd read about Blake Winters, nothing about the man was simple. So why should she expect this to be any different? "What's the catch?"

"You'll have to work at his place."

An ebony eyebrow disappeared beneath the fringe of Savannah's dark bangs. "His place?"

"He's got a house on the Mendocino coast, north of San Francisco."

"The man actually expects me to travel all the way up there, just for an opportunity to audition?"

"He's rather possessive about the film," Justin explained. "He doesn't like to let it out of his sight."

Terrific. She already had the scars to prove what happened when a woman got involved with an overly possessive man. "Perhaps this isn't such a good idea..."

"Blake Winters isn't Jerry Larsen," Justin gently pointed out.

After all these years, Savannah wasn't surprised that Justin could read her mind. "If you mean he's not the kind of man to push a woman through a plate-glass window in a jealous rage, you're probably right," she agreed. "But I still think I'll pass."

"Whatever you want." From his expression, Savannah knew that her longtime agent and friend wanted to argue. She also knew that he had never been one to force her into anything. Which wasn't always a blessing. If she'd only listened to him when he'd cautioned her against getting involved with Jerry...

No. She shook her head, refusing to dwell on the past. That chapter of her life was behind her. Her broken bones had healed, her face had been worked on by the best plastic surgeon in Beverly Hills, and now, a year later, the faint scars were only visible in bright sunlight. Unfortunately, she realized with surprise as she left the restaurant, she'd not yet fully recovered from the emotional wounds Jerry Larsen had inflicted.

A PACIFIC STORM was blowing toward the rugged northern California coast. Dark clouds hovered ominously overhead, the white-capped waves crashed against the granite cliffs. Lost in his own thoughts, Blake Winters failed to notice the increasingly threatening weather. Indeed, a storm of an entirely different kind raged on his chiseled features as he strode along the cliff, cursing Savannah Starr under his breath.

What kind of damn game was the woman playing? In the last twenty of her twenty-six years, she'd made fifteen movies, appeared briefly in two television soap operas, one cable miniseries, and even scored her last film. A workaholic himself, Blake could recognize obsession in others.

After being forced to take the past twelve months off, Savannah must be going crazy. According to the well-greased if admittedly inaccurate gossip mill, she was too badly scarred to ever appear on the screen again. If that were true—and since Justin had alluded to her unwillingness to return to acting, it might well be—the woman had no choice but to turn her attention to her music.

Her father's international fame, while opening some doors, could not guarantee her work. The chances were that she'd be forced to discover firsthand exactly how competitive the music business could be—especially now that modern electronic advances had virtually killed the studio-music scene.

Yet, here he was, offering her a chance to bypass all those closed doors. *Unholy Matrimony* was the best—not to mention the most commercial—film he'd ever made. He needed the right sound track to emphasize the proper mood. His every instinct told him that Savannah Starr was the woman to write that score. So, what had she done? Told her agent, "Thanks, but no thanks," and walked away from a golden—hell, a platinum—opportunity.

Blake Winters was a man used to maintaining control over all aspects of his life. Unfortunately, he'd learned the hard way that controlling the behavior of a single woman was infinitely more difficult than directing a film crew numbering in the hundreds.

"I'll give her three days to change her mind," he muttered into the wind. Jamming his hands into the back pockets of his jeans, he glared out over the storm-tossed sea. "And then I'll just have to change it for her."

SAVANNAH SAT on the balcony of her Malibu home, her bare feet perched on the wooden railing, watching the morning parade of joggers run up and down the beach. She sipped her coffee, willing the caffeine to enter her bloodstream. It was four days after her lunch with Justin, and during that time she doubted that she'd slept more than ten hours. For three restless nights she'd tossed and turned, intrigued by the idea of working closely with Blake Winters, yet feeling equally apprehensive.

Immediately after leaving the restaurant, she'd gone to the *L.A. Times* building, where she'd spent the remainder of the afternoon in the morgue, poring over microfilm of year-old newspaper clippings. While she'd made more than her share of headlines in those days, Blake had been busy creating a few of his own—the most unsettling being those in which the police questioned him regarding his wife's near-fatal car crash.

According to the published reports, his wife had allegedly been having affairs with other men, including a well-known producer whom she ultimately married after a particularly messy divorce. Although no charges had been filed, rumors persisted that Pamela Winters's accident was a failed attempt by Blake Winters to kill his wife for her blatant infidelity.

To Savannah, who'd already suffered at the hands of a dangerously possessive man, such rumors proved chilling. Enough so, that her nightmares had returned with a vengeance, their horrors even infiltrating her waking mind during the day.

She'd returned to the kitchen for a refill when her doorbell rang, jerking her from her unsettling thoughts. Peering through the peephole in the door, she breathed a sigh of relief as she recognized the uniformed courier. Even then, she remained cautious, opening the door only wide enough to accept delivery of the red-and-white cardboard envelope.

After exchanging polite pleasantries about the weather, Savannah shut the door, refastening the multiple locks before turning her attention to the envelope, whose contents were boldly proclaimed in a bright primary red to be Urgent.

"You win this round," the brief note read in a strong, masculine scrawl. "Here are two scenes; you're the only one outside the immediate crew to read them." It was signed, without the bother of a polite closing, simply, "Blake Winters."

Unwillingly intrigued in spite of her better judgment, Savannah took the pages out onto the balcony and began to read. The first scene, glowingly lit by candlelight, depicted the protagonist falling in love; it was lushly romantic, bordering on the erotic.

But if that successfully captured her attention, it was the second scene—where the husband belatedly discovered that he'd married a female vampire—that proved absolutely riveting. Broadly drawn, it borrowed from a mingling of romance, black comedy and horror genres, while remaining both fresh and familiar at the same time.

Ten minutes later, Savannah had finished the sample pages and was eager for more. "I'll say this for you, Winters," she muttered with reluctant admiration, "you have definitely piqued my interest."

At that precise moment, the doorbell sounded again. It was the courier with another envelope. This time, rather than the additional scenes Savannah had been hoping for, Blake Winters had enclosed an airline ticket to San Francisco and another brief note.

"You can view the corresponding clips tomorrow. I'll meet your flight and drive you up the coast to my house. Don't bother to bring any recording equipment; I have everything you'll need." This time he'd merely scrawled his initials at the bottom of the page.

"The nerve of the man," Savannah fumed. "Thinking he can order me around this way." She began pacing the bleached-oak flooring of her living room. "If he treated his wife this way, it's no wonder she fooled around."

No, Savannah amended reluctantly. Even if Blake Winters had acted like a dictator, that didn't excuse Pamela's blatant behavior with other men. Not wanting to prejudge a woman she'd met only once, and then just briefly, Savannah considered that perhaps Pamela had tried to escape her marriage, only to be held captive by her husband's unyielding possessiveness.

Even as she told herself that she wanted nothing to do with such a man, even professionally, Savannah couldn't keep the tantalizing strains of music from her mind. There was no doubt about it; Blake Winters's darkly compelling scenes had effectively stimulated her creativity.

"All right," she muttered, marching into the bedroom where she began throwing clothing into an overnight bag, "I'll audition for your damn movie. But on my terms. And at my convenience."

By the time she landed in San Francisco that afternoon, twenty-four hours ahead of Blake's autocratic schedule, the evocative melodies running through Savannah's mind had almost made her forget her initial aversion to working with such an impossible, dangerous man.

2

IT WAS DUSK, too late for sunlight, too early for stars, by the time Savannah left the highway, following the hand-drawn map that she'd wheedled from Justin. Although she'd expected another hour of daylight, night seemed to come quickly in this part of the country. As she drove through the towering redwood groves, the sky grew darker, the temperature dropped, and ominous drops of rain began splattering against the windshield of her rented car.

"You have got to be crazy," Savannah muttered to herself, leaning forward over the steering wheel to peer out into the widening well of purple darkness. The wind picked up and the rain began to slant hard. "How do you know he'll even be home?"

If she had any sense, Savannah told herself, she would have stopped at that friendly-looking inn a few miles back and telephoned him. But she had been overtaken by some perverse desire to arrive unannounced, to demonstrate unequivocally that even the great Blake Winters couldn't always have things *his* way.

But with the way this road was beginning to wash out, if she arrived to find the man not at home, she could very easily end up spending the night in her car.

Which was, considering the potential of the Pacific storm brewing outside, a most unappealing scenario.

Savannah had never considered herself a reckless person. She'd always left the flamboyant behavior and caution-throwing to her famous parents. During this past year, she'd grown even more prudent, and although she refused to accept Justin's accusation that she was hiding behind the multiple locks on her house, she couldn't deny that it had been a very long time since she'd ventured more than a few miles from home. And then, only during the day, when the bright California sunshine illuminated everything and everyone, making her feel almost safe.

So, what was she doing, traveling alone on this treacherous mountain road, headed toward the home of a man she knew little about, other than the fact that he was rumored to have tried to kill his wife?

"Don't be ridiculous." Her voice sounded unnaturally loud in the close confines of the car. "Those were only vicious tabloid rumors. Nothing more. Besides, Justin would never have encouraged you to work with the man if he thought you'd be in any danger."

Terrific. Now she was talking to herself. Nothing like a north-coast storm to drive a person a little insane. No wonder Winters had written a screenplay about a vampire. The man definitely lived in the right place for it.

The rain fell harder, streaming down the windshield, making visibility nearly impossible. Although she hated to admit to what she considered a distressingly feminine weakness, storms had always played havoc with her nerves. And tonight was no exception.

Darkness engulfed the car. Her senses were so stimulated by the building storm that Savannah began to imagine that the black tree limbs arching over the narrow roadway were ominously gesturing arms, leading her into danger. All the eerie atmosphere needed was the howl of a werewolf—or the flapping of a vampire's black-caped wings.

She considered going back, but common sense told her that if she tried to turn the car around on this narrow gravel road, she'd only succeed in getting mired down in the muddy shoulder. No, she had no choice but to continue on the path she'd chosen.

Five minutes later, she drove through a particularly deep wash. Moments later, the engine coughed and shuddered to a stop.

"Damn!"

Savannah twisted the key in the ignition. Once. Twice. Forcing herself to count to ten, she tried a third time. But there was only a weak grinding sound that gave way to an ominous silence.

"Damn Blake Winters's black heart," she cursed, slamming her hands down on the steering wheel. This was, without a doubt, the most stupid thing she'd ever done. But now that she'd come this far...

She turned on the dome light and studied the map. If the map was accurate, she was less than half a mile from Winters's house. Before her near-fatal fall through her living-room window, she'd run ten times that distance each morning before breakfast.

Heaving a sigh, she tried the ignition one last time. Nothing. Pocketing the key with another curse, she left the car. As she trudged up the muddy road, bent against the driving wind, Savannah prayed that Blake Winters was at home.

HE WAS. While Savannah was slowly making her way toward his rambling Victorian house, Blake was sitting in front of a comfortable fire, watching her slink across his large-screen television set, clad in a clinging white silk slip that displayed every lush curve to advantage.

Cut to a close-up. Her thickly lashed eyes, the color of rich, dark coffee, were guileless as she coaxed her married lover into committing murder. Although Blake, more than most men, understood the difference between real life and the movies, when those wide eyes looked directly at him, he experienced a slow, seductive pull—the same painfully erotic pull he'd been suffering for days.

Cursing, he pointed the remote control at the television and darkened the screen. Pushing himself out of the chair, he walked over to the bank of windows and watched the flashes of lightning arc over the darkening sea.

He'd always enjoyed living on this part of the coast; he found the storms exciting, invigorating—unlike Pamela, who'd complained that the wind and rain destroyed her expensively coiffed blond hair and that between the morning fog and the afternoon rains, it was utterly impossible to get a decent tan.

His wife had much preferred Beverly Hills, which Blake hated. Which was why, after the initial whirlwind courtship, he'd reluctantly agreed to separate homes.

In the beginning, the plan had been for him to write during the week, here on the coast, and for her to join him on the weekends. And when his wife's busy social calendar began to preclude such visits, he'd tried visiting her in that outrageously expensive French Regency manor that he considered more a museum than a proper home.

But the house was always packed to the rafters with guests, and the weekends consisted of elaborate brunches by the pool, excruciatingly boring society lunches, and formal dinner parties where the guests tried to outdo each other with their sartorial splendor. By the sixth month of their marriage, Blake found the atmosphere increasingly claustrophobic—a complaint Pamela blithely dismissed.

An intense lightning flash preceded a stunning roll of thunder. The lights flickered briefly, then went out, plunging the house into darkness. Retrieving a book of matches from the desk drawer, Blake went around the room lighting the candles he kept for just such an emergency. After dealing with that little domestic problem, he allowed his mind to drift back to his disastrous marriage.

It hadn't been easy on his ego to admit that he'd made a mistake—that he'd fallen in love with the woman Pamela had pretended to be, rather than the self-consumed, frighteningly ambitious actress who'd do anything to get a part—including marrying a man in order to coax him into writing a screenplay she could use as a vehicle for fame and fortune.

Even as she constantly derided him for what she considered his boring, rustic life-style, Pamela had refused to give him a divorce. There were definite perks to being Mrs. Blake Winters—privileges she was not about to give up. By the time their second anniversary rolled around, they were living in mutual distaste, miles from each other.

Blake's fingers tightened around his glass. That was all in the past; he'd exorcised his deep, seething anger while writing *Unholy Matrimony*. The film was the most autobiographical and the best work he'd ever done. After viewing the rough cut, Justin had agreed, predicting that Blake would not only walk away with all the awards at Cannes, but sweep the Oscars, as well. So, why the hell was he in such a rotten mood?

It was because of her. Savannah Starr. Oh, he had no doubt that Justin was right about her ability to score his film; after hearing the sound track from her last film, Blake realized that she'd inherited her father's musical genius. What he did have a great many questions about was his ability to work closely with such a beautiful woman. Or, at least, one as beautiful as she had once been. Because he had the scars to prove that a woman, too, could hide one helluva lot behind such wide, guileless eyes. Furious at letting Savannah get under his skin before she'd even arrived, Blake poured himself another drink and brooded.

FINALLY! Savannah could have wept with relief when she reached Blake Winters's cliffside house. But when she actually focused on the huge Gothic mansion, complete with a tower and widow's walk, her breath caught in her throat.

The stone house was draped in deep purple shadows that served to intensify its brooding atmosphere. And although it reminded her of the type of home Dracula might have chosen, were the vampire to decide to relocate from Transylvania to northern California, it was, she told herself, a safe, warm refuge from the storm. As if to push her inside, the rain came down even harder, and lighting washed the house in brief, stuttering flashes of light.

The lion's-head knocker was heavy and old. After banging it against the ornately carved door for what seemed like hours, Savannah was forced to face her worst fear: that Winters wasn't home. She had just decided to break one of the darkened windows to gain entrance to the house, when the heavy door swung open to reveal Dracula himself, silhouetted by a flare of lightning.

No. Not Dracula, she determined on a cooling rush of relief. The storm had caused her imagination to run amok. It was only Winters, clad in black jeans and a black sweater. Not that he looked all that safe, himself. His jet-black hair was swept back from a deep widow's peak and his stormy eyes were either black or brown—she couldn't quite tell which. His features, illuminated by the flickering candle he held in his left hand, appeared to have been chiseled from a block of granite. "What the hell are you doing here?" Brows lowered, he stared down at her.

Irritation and exhaustion steamrolled her earlier fear. "Unless my memory has failed, I believe you ordered me here," she shot back.

"I was expecting you tomorrow."

"I know. But I was so excited about the chance to collaborate with genius that I couldn't resist coming early." She flashed him a patently false smile.

"How did you get here?"

"How do you think? I drove."

"In this weather?" He glanced past her. "Where's your car?"

"It's down the road about half a mile. I think it drowned in that last wash I had to cross."

His fathomless eyes met hers with no change of expression. "You walked all that way?" That explained why her sweater and jeans were soaked. As annoyed as he was by her unexpected arrival, Blake couldn't help noticing how nicely those snug jeans hugged her hips.

"I was going to wait for a tow truck—" Savannah pushed her dripping hair out of her eyes "—but none showed up."

"Well, I suppose now that you're here, you may as well come in out of the rain," he decided.

"Gee," she drawled, "I've always heard about northern-California hospitality, but it's so illuminating to see it in action."

"And here I thought I was on my best behavior."

Refusing to answer such an outrageous statement, her chin high and her eyes flashing, Savannah swept past him into the vast dark foyer. There wasn't a light burning anywhere in the house; it was as black and silent as a tomb. "So where are the rest of the vampires?"

Although she amused him, Blake managed, with effort, to keep the humor from his face. "Out getting their nightly ration of blood."

Knowing that she was behaving abominably, but unable to stop herself, Savannah asked, "Why aren't you out with them?"

"I was waiting for you."

Blake wished that he could see her face more clearly. The candle offered only a faint, flickering light, but even with her dark hair a wet tangle over her shoulders, Savannah Starr was every bit as stunning in person as she'd been on the movie screen. And as sexy as in his dreams.

He was looking at her closely. Too closely. Savannah resisted the impulse to cover her scarred cheek with her palm. "You might have had a long wait."

He regarded her obliquely for a long, silent time. "No," he said finally. "I knew you'd come."

Savannah realized that she should be furious at his arrogant attitude. But the frustrating thing was that he was right. "I almost didn't. I'm not accustomed to auditioning."

He nodded. "So Justin said. But I thought it was important that I see how we work together."

Savannah's eyes widened. "That's what this is all about? To see if we're compatible?"

"Not exactly." He turned and headed toward a floating staircase with an ornately carved mahogany banister. "You'll want to get out of those wet things," he said. "I'll show you to your room."

Unwilling to let the faint flare of the candle out of her sight, Savannah followed close on his heels. Something brushed against her legs; she pressed her fingers against her lips to stifle a scream. Relief rushed over her when she viewed the midnight-black cat at her feet. "What do you mean, 'Not exactly'?"

"It's a bit complicated to explain. And you've had a tiring drive." He reached the landing and waited for her to catch up before continuing.

"I'm not that tired."

Blake appeared not to have heard her. "Your room is right down the hall." Although Savannah had always prided herself on her long legs, she found herself hurrying to keep up with his lengthy stride. "Have you eaten?"

"Some peanuts on the plane."

"That's hardly eating." He stopped in front of a closed door. "After you get settled in, I'll fix you a light supper. How does soup and sandwiches sound?"

"I thought the electricity was out." Surely he didn't keep the house this dark because he preferred it that way? she considered. Even a man with Blake Winters's maverick reputation couldn't be that weird.

"I had a backup wood stove installed in the kitchen. The power goes out a lot up here, and I like to cook."

"Oh." The idea of this mysteriously intimidating man puttering around a kitchen strained even Savannah's vivid imagination. "I'm surprised you don't have a housekeeper to do that."

"I like my solitude." He slanted her a mocking look. "If you're afraid to spend the night alone in this house with me, we can call Justin and have him assure you that I'm not a serial killer, or a rapist."

"If the electricity is out, the phone probably isn't working, either," she said.

"Good point." He gave her a brief, savage smile. "Then I suppose you'll just have to trust me, won't you?"

She'd just as soon trust the devil. But then she reassured herself yet again that Justin wouldn't have encouraged her to come here if Winters was even half as dangerous as he looked.

"I suppose I will," she agreed stiffly. "And as for supper, it's very nice of you to offer, Mr. Winters, but it isn't necessary."

"I insist. After all, we can't have you swooning from hunger your first night here, can we?"

His words indicated that he believed that there would be more than one night. Determined to set the record straight, Savannah followed him into the room. "I'll be returning to Los Angeles tomorrow afternoon."

"Don't be ridiculous. We won't be finished with the audition by then." Ignoring her angry intake of breath, he went around the room, lighting a variety of fragrant white beeswax candles.

"I already know what I want to do with those scenes," she insisted. "So long as you've got a synthesizer and a computer, I should be able to give you an idea what I have in mind by noon tomorrow, at the latest."

"I'm impressed by your forethought, Ms. Starr, but that still won't be enough time. Wait here. I'll be right back."

He left the room, returning momentarily with a thick terry-cloth robe that he tossed onto the bed. The robe, which Savannah assumed was his, was black, adding to the impression of Blake Winters as a creature of the night. She found herself wishing she'd thought to pack a garlic necklace. Or was that for werewolves? She definitely should have paid more attention to Christopher Lee's Dracula films.

"The bathroom's right through that door," he said. "I imagine you're in the mood for a long hot shower about now."

A hot shower sounded heavenly. But, immersed in her exacerbation, Savannah refused to succumb to his enticing suggestion. "I hate to get into artistic differences right off the bat," she said stiffly. "But you're wrong. One day is definitely enough time to show you how I've interpreted your scenes. Talent doesn't answer to a time clock, Mr. Winters. You, of all people, should know that."

"I wasn't referring to your talent, Ms. Starr," he returned smoothly. "I realized the first time I heard your work that you're incredibly gifted."

"So, why am I here?"

Blake's answer was short and sweet. It was also the last thing Savannah expected to hear. "So I can discover whether or not I can work with you without taking you to bed."

With that, he was gone, leaving her to sink down onto the soft feather mattress and stare after him.

BLAKE SIPPED thoughtfully on his drink as he heated the hearty minestrone and sliced last night's roast into thick sandwiches. In the background, the portable kitchen radio was tuned to a San Francisco blues station.

The lady definitely wasn't a pushover. And although he was not accustomed to people questioning his authority, Blake couldn't help but admire her spunk. Most women of his acquaintance, after trudging through rain and mud, would have burst into tears if met with the same unwelcoming attitude with which he'd greeted her.

He knew that if she reported his behavior back to Justin, his longtime friend and agent would probably feel obliged to deck him, just on principle. But something told him that Savannah would keep their little altercation to herself; she was definitely a woman willing to fight her own battles. Which proved how deceptive appearances could be.

He was slicing tomatoes for a salad, remembering how deceptively vulnerable she'd looked, standing on his front porch, dripping wet, when her soft voice broke into his thoughts.

"Did you actually mean what you said? About us going to bed?"

She was engulfed in folds of black terry cloth. Her hair, though combed, hung in wet tangles over her shoulders; beads of water gleamed on her ivory skin, revealed by the robe's neckline. The plastic surgeons had done a remarkable job on her still-exquisite face. Although it might have been a trick of the softly flattering light from the candle she carried, Blake couldn't see any scars. Her feet were bare, the polish on her toenails gleaming like pink seashells. Desire hit him hard.

Forcing it down with a frown, Blake returned to slicing the tomatoes. "If we end up working together, you'll discover that I never say anything I don't mean."

"Mr. Winters—"

"It's Blake."

Determined to get control of the situation, Savannah ignored his murmured suggestion. "Mr. Winters," she said forcefully, "I cannot believe that you are so desperate for a woman that you'd bring me all the way up here to seduce me." The cat, which had remained with her while she showered and dressed, wove figure eights between her ankles, purring thickly.

He glanced up at her with polite curiosity. "Do you feel in danger of being seduced?"

Thinking that he'd been barely civil since her arrival, Savannah was forced to answer honestly: "Hardly."

He shrugged. "Then I suggest you not worry. When and if I decide to seduce you, Savannah," he said, his eyes lifting to hers, holding her unwilling gaze by the sheer strength of his will, "believe me, you'll know."

Savannah shook her head. "You're a very strange man," she murmured, watching with fascination at the skill in which he wielded the razor-sharp knife.

"So I've been told. How was your shower?" he asked. "Did you have enough hot water?"

"You can't change the subject just like that," she complained.

"Of course I can. You know, I'm surprised you found your way down here by yourself. The house has a lot of twists and turns."

Savannah's frustrated sigh ruffled her bangs. Obviously Winters was determined to control the conversation. Recognizing tenacity when she saw it, Savannah decided not to respond to his obvious attempts to initiate an argument. She'd be as polite and agreeable as possible. Tomorrow morning, she'd play him the score that had been haunting her mind for hours, and then be on her way. Back to Malibu. To her own home. And her own life.

"I got lost twice," she admitted. "Finally I decided to follow your cat. If it wasn't for him, I probably would have spent the rest of my life wandering these halls like some ancient ghost."

"You should have stayed where you were. I intended to bring dinner up to you."

"Actually, it was rather exciting," she said with a faint smile. "I felt like a character in one of those old horror movies. I almost expected to disappear behind a sliding panel."

"It's been known to happen," Blake agreed. He didn't know why Savannah was suddenly being so cheerful, but he had a feeling that if he waited long enough, he'd find out what she was up to. "There was a guy up here six months ago trying to sell me aluminium siding. He went into the library to write up his quote and I haven't seen him since."

Savannah thought she saw a glimmer of a smile in his eyes, but decided that it had to be a trick of the candlelight. "Can I help?"

"I have everything under control."

Which was just the way he liked things, Savannah mused. Biting down on her building frustration, she tried another track. "If the rest of the scenes of your movie are half as good as the ones you've sent me, you've got yourself a hit," she said conversationally, watching him chop fragrant green leaves of fresh basil with quick, sure strokes.

"House rules—no business talk with meals. It leads to indigestion and ruins the efforts of the cook." He waved the knife in the direction of the refrigerator. "If you really want to help, you'll find some wine in there. How are you with a corkscrew?"

Savannah was frustrated by his refusal to discuss his work, but, not wanting to rock what appeared to be a dangerously precarious boat, she padded over to the refrigerator and located the wine.

"I'm surprised at how warm it is in here." She'd been worried about not having any dry shoes to put on after her shower, but the floor had proved remarkably warm.

"The house is built on an underground hot spring," Blake divulged. "When the first owner built the house, back at the turn of the century, he put in a steam boiler."

He sprinkled the chopped basil over the tomato slices. "When I bought the place, the realtor warned that I'd have to dig a new well and put in a modern heating system, but so far, that old boiler just keeps kicking out the heat."

"Lucky," Savannah said. She watched him work with a smooth, precise, patient skill that she couldn't help but admire. Patience had never been her strong suit, and although she'd tried on several occasions to learn to cook, inevitably her mind would drift during some crucial stage and she'd end, at best, with a ruined meal; at worst, with a kitchen filled with smoke and firemen.

"I thought so." Blake drizzled a honey-mustard vinaigrette over the tomatoes.

"Actually," Savannah admitted, "when I first arrived, I thought this place was pretty spooky." She glanced around the rustic kitchen, taking in the copper pots and the lush green plants. "But the candlelight is rather nice."

Here it was—the seductive, let's-get-to-know-each-other pitch. Then later, when she'd softened him up sufficiently, it would be time for her to suggest that she was the only person who understood him enough to appreciate his work. As sexy as Savannah admittedly was, Blake was disappointed to discover that she was no different from so many other women of his acquaintance. Pamela included. *Especially* Pamela.

He put the salads on the table, along with a platter of sandwiches and the tureen of thick minestrone. "Most women would probably consider candlelight romantic, I suppose."

Savannah looked up from pouring the wine, puzzled by his suddenly gritty tone. For a few minutes, she'd begun to believe that they'd simply gotten off to a bad start; that if they both tried, they might be able to get along.

"I said 'nice,'" she reminded him quietly. "Not romantic."

"Whatever."

He held the chair out for her. Savannah hesitated, then sat down, wondering if he was going to continue to glower at her all through dinner.

3

FORTUNATELY, whatever had been bothering Blake seemed to pass, allowing them to eat in reasonably companionable silence, enjoying the bluesy tones of Marvin Gaye in the background.

Savannah found the minestrone delicious and was less surprised than she might have been when he revealed that he'd made it himself last week. The sandwiches were thick, piled high with roast beef and Swiss cheese on sourdough bread. The light vinaigrette dressing on the tomatoes was expertly seasoned. Was there anything this man couldn't do? Savannah wondered.

Later, when he suggested having their brandy upstairs in his den, she felt too satiated and at ease to recognize the trap.

"Oh! It's wonderful," she exclaimed as he led her into the octagonal tower room.

A bank of undraped ceiling-high windows allowed a three-hundred-and-sixty-degree view of the storm that continued to rage outside, splitting the night sky with brilliant, jagged lightning. Drawn by the magnificent scene, Savannah walked over to the windows. From way, way down below, she could hear the distant sound of the surf crashing against the granite cliffs.

Blake watched the enchantment shining in her eyes and wondered if she was acting. The first time Pamela had set foot in this room, she had complained that it reminded her of the torture chamber in a horror movie. That said, she'd refused ever to put her dainty little size-four feet across the doorway again.

"How odd," Savannah said. "I usually hate storms." She was standing in front of the bank of windows, looking out over the storm-tossed sea. "But up here, it's different." Thunder boomed. Lighting flashed like a thousand strobe lights, bathing the room in blinding white light. "It's thrilling." She tossed Blake a dazzling smile over her shoulder. "I feel like Thor."

The excitement in her eyes caused a rush of arousal to surge, unwanted, through his system. "This room is the reason I bought the house."

"I can see why."

Sighing appreciatively, Savannah left the windows, sank onto the soft black leather couch and put her bare feet up on the granite table. The cat settled on the Oriental rug in front of the fire and began washing its paws. The crackling fire in the stone fireplace gave off a warm glow, along with a pungent scent of cedar.

"I envy you. Living here would be like being in the middle of a fairy tale. I can almost see Rapunzel lowering her hair to her prince."

When her smile warmed him to the core, Blake decided that while Savannah's seduction methods might be a great deal less sophisticated than Pamela's had been, they were no less fatal.

In the beginning, Pamela had called him her Prince
Charming. Like a fool, he'd tried like hell to live up to
the role. In the beginning, anyway....

"I've never been a fan of fairy tales."

His dark eyes iced over, reminding Savannah that
cold could be every bit as dangerous as heat. "Actually," she said, "neither have I. My father used to read
me the Brothers Grimm when I was a little girl. It always seemed that the princesses had long, flowing
blond locks, while the ugly witches all had black hair.
I hated that."

Melanie Raine had been famous for her long platinum waves. Blake wondered idly if Savannah had felt
the need to compete with her ultraglamorous mother.

"Snow White was a brunette," he pointed out.

"Do you know, all those years, I never once thought
of Snow White," Savannah admitted. "Where were you
when I was six years old?"

Her soft laugh reminded Blake of crystal wind-
chimes in a soft summer breeze. His unwilling response to that laugh annoyed him. "Not hanging
around Beverly Hills, that's for damn sure."

Savannah thought she detected sarcasm in his tone.
"Don't tell me that a man whose last picture grossed
twenty million dollars in the opening weekend, actually resents those of us who happened to have been born
rich?"

"Of course not," he said, not quite truthfully. So she
was perceptive, as well as being talented and beautiful. Blake found the combination vaguely threatening.
Frowning, he poured some Courvoisier into a pair of
snifters and handed one to her.

"To a successful collaboration."

She looked up at him, puzzled. "I didn't think that was settled yet."

Sitting down beside her, he gave her a smile that didn't quite reach his shuttered eyes. "I didn't want to give you the job until I proved to myself that I could resist sleeping with you." Ignoring Savannah's furious gasp, he sipped his cognac thoughtfully. "But over dinner I decided that I was being ridiculous."

Savannah didn't bother to hide her relief. "I'm so glad you came to that decision," she said. "Because I really want to score your film."

"I know."

Placing his glass slowly, deliberately, on the coffee table, he turned toward her. Her mouth, curved in a smile, looked very soft and very tempting. For countless hours over these past nights, Savannah's image and his own vivid imagination had tormented him relentlessly.

Although he'd fought against it, the arousal he'd been feeling since first screening her film and listening to her sultry, seductive score, returned to taunt him yet again. This time Blake decided to satisfy it.

His hand slipped under her drying hair and cupped her neck. "I vowed that I wasn't going to fall victim to your seductive spell."

Blake's eyes didn't waver from hers as he slowly traced the shape of her mouth with his thumb. When her lips trembled apart, he lowered his head, his intent obvious.

"But then when you showed up in my kitchen, looking like some delectable mermaid who'd washed up on my shore, I decided, what the hell."

Savannah couldn't think, much less move or speak. Before she could dredge up a single word of protest, his lips covered hers in a slow, drugging kiss that sent her head spinning. Her fingers tightened on her glass; the breath she'd been unaware of holding shuddered out. His clever tongue softly teased its way between her lips, feathering against hers in a way that made her go numb from the knees down.

There was no artifice in her kiss, no clever expertise. As her arms crept around his neck and she pressed her slender body against his, Blake could feel the aching need in her—or was it his own need? Even as he tried to remind himself that as an actress, Savannah Starr was more than capable of feigning both innocence and passion, a rebellious part of his mind pointed out that there was something unique in the way her mouth fit his. And somehow he knew that if he took her now, it wouldn't be easy to walk away.

Part of Savannah's brain realized that she was suddenly completely vulnerable, that she should resist the spell he was spinning around them. But her mind was becoming wrapped in a velvet fog; her blood warmed, her pulse hummed. As impossible as it sounded, she was floating. How could that be? As he deepened the kiss, degree by aching degree, coherent thought disintegrated. She sighed—a whisper of sound against his mouth.

It was taking every ounce of Blake's willpower not to rip off the bulky robe and bury himself in her warm, welcoming heat. Passion raged in him. He felt an al-most-savage urge to plunder; he wanted to devour Sa-vannah Starr almost as much as he wanted to savor her.

"Dammit. You win, mermaid," he growled against her throat. "The job's all yours."

His grim words were like a splash of ice water on her swirling senses. Pushing against his shoulders, Savan-nah broke away. "I can't believe you think . . ."

Savannah took a deep breath, dragging both hands through her hair as she tried to articulate her outrage. She knew that she would always—for as long as she lived—hate herself for succumbing to that stolen mo-ment of golden pleasure.

Plying her talent for all it was worth, she tossed her head and gave him a cool, withering look. "For your information, Mr. Winters, the casting couch went out with twenty-five-cent popcorn, newsreels and double features."

Blake's implacable gaze drifted to her unfettered breasts, heaving beneath the terry cloth. The Lady As-tor routine was an act, he determined. But her temper was honest, even if he was at a loss to understand why she was so angry.

"You've got the job, Savannah. Why quibble about the whys and hows?" The warmth she'd felt in Blake's kiss was missing from his eyes.

Savannah wanted to tell him that she wouldn't score his horrid film even if he groveled—if he crawled on his hands and knees over broken glass. But then she thought about those wonderful, vivid scenes and de-cided that to turn her back on such a golden opportu-nity, simply because Blake Winters was a egotistical, male-chauvinist playboy who couldn't resist anything in skirts, would be a classic case of cutting off her nose to spite her face.

Outside, lightning ripped across the night sky as she forced herself to meet his shuttered gaze with a calm she was a very long way from feeling.

"You seem to be under the impression that I came all this way, slogging through mud and rain, to sleep with you."

He retrieved his glass from the coffee table, cupped it between his palms and slowly swirled the amber cognac. "Didn't you?" he asked laconically.

Her cool pretense slipped. Savannah stared at him. "Of course not! No more than you intended to sleep with me."

"But I do." His voice, while low, was deadly. "I thought I'd made that quite obvious."

She looked as if she'd been struck. Her eyes were wide and uncharacteristically vulnerable; her face was pale. "But you don't even know me."

"Of course I do."

She swallowed, but her throat stayed dry. "We've never met."

"True. But I've spent the past two weeks screening your last film. Over and over again."

"That doesn't count. I was playing a character who was nothing like me." Dear Lord, Savannah considered, surely Blake didn't think she was anything like that oversexed black widow she'd portrayed in *Seduced*. He, of all people, should be able to distinguish between a movie and real life. *Shouldn't he?*

"I realize that. I was talking about the sound track." His eyes left hers to settle on her softly parted lips. Lips he could still taste. "It told me everything about you, Savannah."

"That's ridiculous," she insisted raggedly. Even as she denied his outrageous statement, Savannah found herself remembering her mother's complaint, years after the divorce, that the only way she'd ever been able to remotely know what Savannah's father had been thinking or feeling was through his music.

"Is it?" His hand cupped her chin, gently holding her hostage. "I know that you're a woman who made a near-fatal mistake by choosing the wrong man."

He frightened her. She didn't know him, she couldn't understand his mind or his motives. There was a great deal of violence in his movies. Was there violence in the man?

"Anyone who reads *People* magazine, or the *Enquirer*, knows that." Success. Her voice was calm and steady. Unlike her runaway pulse.

"But do those readers know how passionate you are?" he wondered aloud. "Do they realize the hidden depths lurking beneath that smooth, polite exterior?"

His eyes on hers, he trailed his hand down her throat, lingering against her pulse beat, which leaped in response to his touch. "Do they know that your flesh warms when I touch you here?" When his wicked fingers blazed a trail across the skin revealed by the rolled collar of the oversize robe, something soft, something warm, flowed through her. "Or here?"

Other than a multitude of doctors, no man had touched her in over a year. As she felt herself succumbing to the seductive heat of his caress, Savannah told herself that she should be grateful to Blake Winters for stimulating feelings that she thought had died. It had been so long, Savannah mused as her warming body warred with her mind. Too long.

Frustrated and furious and desperately needing to distance herself and regain some small measure of control, she broke away and went over to the bank of windows, where she stood looking out over the wine-dark sea.

Blake stretched his legs out in front of him, leaned back and watched her silently. She had her arms wrapped around herself, in an unconscious gesture of self-protection. Engulfed as she was in the too-large robe, she suddenly looked very small. And very vulnerable. Something in his heart moved. Frowning, he steeled himself against it.

Neither of them said anything for a long, silent time. But Savannah knew, without turning around, that he was watching her through those dangerously narrowed, dark eyes. As for Blake, it didn't take mind-reading ability to know that Savannah was thinking about him. And about the devastating kiss they'd shared.

He'd wanted her, and for that, Blake refused to apologize. Desire was familiar, comfortable. Hell, even normal. What was disturbing was the sudden depth of that desire—along with something new, something alien; something that had felt uncomfortably like need.

"This isn't ever going to work," she said finally, more to herself than to him.

"Probably not," he agreed.

Savannah spun around, pinning him with an accusing glare. The firelight danced on his arrogant, controlled features. How dare he remain so calm when she was not? She balled her hands into fists and plunged then deep into the pockets of the robe.

"I know I've only done one sound track, but I'm the best person you'll find to score *Unholy Matrimony*."

Although he was intrigued by the flame in her eyes, Blake's expression gave nothing away. "You're perfect."

His easy answer surprised her. As had everything else about this man. "I don't understand."

"That makes two of us." He rose from the couch and crossed the room, stopping directly in front of her. "It's late. And you've had a long flight and a harrowing drive. Why don't we talk about all this tomorrow?"

His suggestion had merit, but Savannah found herself disliking the way that he was once again manipulating things to his own satisfaction. "Are you always this bossy?"

"So I've been told. Are you always this obstinate?"

"So *I've* been told."

Blake rubbed his chin; a small smile played at the corners of his mouth. "This could be a very interesting collaboration."

Savannah decided that she rather liked the way little lines crinkled at the corners of his eyes when he smiled. For a fleeting moment, she felt that perhaps there was a chance they could work together, after all.

"Or a disastrous one," he tacked on.

Beginning to understand how he operated, Savannah refused to let him bait her. "You'll never know unless you try," she suggested sweetly.

Blake nodded thoughtfully. "True enough." His gaze swept over her, from her hair—shining like polished ebony in the glow of the firelight—to her gleaming pink toenails. "Tomorrow morning you'll show me what you've planned."

"Fine."

"How does five-thirty sound?"

"Like the middle of the night."

"I like to get an early start."

"Good for you," she countered silkily. "But at five-thirty, you'll do it without me."

He folded his arms over his chest. "Six?"

"What do you have against working in the daylight?"

His dark eyes were fixed on her face. Savannah found herself wishing for daylight, so she could determine their true color. "Everyone knows that we vampires do our best work in the dark."

She had the grace to blush. "I'm sorry. That really was uncalled for," she admitted.

The color rose in her cheeks like the bloom of late-summer roses, making Blake's fingers practically itch to touch their velvety softness. Determined not to be lured into her tender trap, he forced a nonchalant shrug.

"You were cold and wet, and this house can be a little intimidating. Especially at night."

And most especially when she was greeted by a man who was a dead ringer for Count Dracula, Savannah tacked on mentally. Even now, when he appeared to be trying to make peace, she still found Blake Winters's compelling masculine power more than a little intimidating.

"So long as you've got a pot of coffee close at hand, I suppose I could be ready for work by seven-thirty," she said with a definite lack of enthusiasm.

She was exhausted. He could see it in the fatigue lacing her wide eyes, in the slight slump of her slender shoulders. Blake decided that it would be in his own best interests to be generous.

"The coffee will be ready whenever you get up," he allowed.

Savannah looked at him curiously, wondering what had precipitated this sudden reversal. "That's very nice of you."

"It's not nice at all," Blake replied mildly. "Since I need you at your creative best, it only makes sense to let you get a decent night's sleep."

She should have known better than to expect any compassion from this man. Savannah tilted her chin and met his unreadable gaze with an icy one of her one. "Speaking of sleep, I think I'd like to go to bed now."

He inclined his head. "Good idea," he drawled. Giving in to temptation, he touched her. It was just a hand to her hair, nothing more, but in the midst of the storm raging around them, the gesture seemed incredibly intimate.

Savannah ordered herself to remain calm. "Alone."

Good. Her voice was cool, steady, belying the reckless turmoil inside her. Savannah tried to forget that in every Hollywood remake of the vampire story since

Bram Stoker's memorable novel, Dracula always got any woman he wanted.

She shook her head in an attempt to clear it, reminding herself that despite having grown up in a town built on fantasy and illusion, she was a sensible, down-to-earth woman who had never believed in ghosts, werewolves, vampires, or anything even remotely paranormal.

Blake accepted her refusal without comment. "I'll take you to your room."

Although the last thing Savannah wanted was to allow this man into her bedroom, she also knew that she'd never find her way back to that guest room without his guidance.

She stayed close beside him as they walked through the gloomy, twisting hallways. When they finally reached her room, Savannah was surprised when Blake behaved like a true gentleman, stopping outside the door.

"Good night, Savannah. I'll be looking forward to tomorrow."

"Well, that makes one of us."

At her flippant tone, his piercing eyes filled with questions—as well as a look of suspicion she'd seen there before.

"A surprising answer, Savannah." His hand curled around the nape of her neck, drawing her closer until their lips were only a whisper apart. "But you're a surprising woman." His fingers kneaded her neck. "Perhaps that's why you excite me," he murmured, more to himself than to her.

Longings, needs, desires—all sprang free in her again. Fighting them, Savannah stiffened. She sucked in her breath, vowing to remain cool, detached. But when his lips brushed against hers, detachment quickly turned into longing, denial into need, as all sensation—arousal, a lifetime of passion—became centered on her mouth.

When he caught her bottom lip between his teeth and tugged, Savannah shuddered. When he moved his mouth from hers to the arch of her throat, a moan of pleasure escaped her lips. Even as she fought against it, Savannah was caught in a blinding swirl of longing that had her clinging desperately to his shoulders.

Greed. Hunger. Need. They rose like ancient demons, battering at his insides. Never had Blake felt such intense pain. He pressed her against him, body to body, and his heat seeped into her, melting her last vestiges of resistance. He knew that it would be an easy thing to take Savannah now, while she was caught up in the urgency of the moment. But he wanted more from Savannah Starr than mere sexual gratification. Much, much more.

If he took her to bed now, the first thing she'd do tomorrow morning would be to run back down the mountain to the safety of her Malibu home, leaving his film without a score. Which was one more problem than he could handle.

Due to bad weather and, Blake reluctantly admitted, his own unyielding perfectionism that made him shoot a scene ten times when three would have been sufficient, *Unholy Matrimony* was over budget and dangerously behind schedule. Once, that wouldn't have mattered. Back in the days when studios were run by people who loved movies and whose first concerns were creating films that people would enjoy.

But these days things were different. The entire industry had been taken over by the money-counters— unimaginative, clonelike accountants. Individuals who were only interested in the bottom line. Profits, not originality, were the engine that ran this new and frightening Hollywood machine. And the board of the international conglomerate—headed up by a Japanese car company—who'd taken over his studio during the filming of *Unholy Matrimony*, were even more cost-conscious than most.

They'd already threatened to take the processed film, along with the negative, and put someone less critical—someone willing to rush the creative process, sacrificing style for speed—in charge of the final mix.

He knew exactly what they'd do: hire a talentless hack to churn out some lousy elevator music and track it into the film, whether it fit the mood of each scene or not.

Postproduction was the most crucial period in a film's creation; it was where mediocre movies could be made acceptable—or brilliant ones killed. And he damn well wasn't going to let the Philistines murder *Unholy Matrimony*. Which was why he'd sneaked the edited film out of the studio one night and brought it here, where it couldn't accidentally "disappear."

When the studio executives had found out what he'd done, they'd hit the roof. They'd threatened Blake with lawsuits, pointing out the critical paragraphs in his contract that gave the studio the right to take control of the film. Refusing to be intimidated, Blake had told the outraged executives that he'd rather burn the negative than let them get their greedy hands on it.

His lawyer, more temperamentally suited to negotiation than Blake, had diplomatically suggested that, since Blake was one of the few truly bankable writer/directors in town, the studio give him a little more time to spin his magic. After all, a blockbuster could easily wipe out the overage in its opening weekend.

Only slightly mollified, the studio executives had weighed the chance of a blockbuster movie against a crazy man's threat to destroy nine months'—and millions of dollars'—worth of work, and reluctantly agreed to give Blake more time.

They gave him exactly four weeks. And although only one of those weeks had passed, the damn wolves were already howling at his door; if he didn't have the film ready for release in twenty-one short days, he'd lose control—something he wasn't about to let happen. Slowly, reluctantly, he released Savannah.

Her head still whirling, Savannah drew back, aroused and alarmed by how helpless she'd felt. She stared at Blake in horror, her words stuck in her throat. But before she could summon up an appropriately vile curse, he turned on his booted heel and strode down the hallway, disappearing into the shadows.

Ill at ease and not trusting Blake Winters, Savannah locked the bedroom door behind her. Knowing that she was being paranoid—after all, the bedroom was on the third floor—she also checked to make certain that the window and the French doors leading out to the widow's walk were locked, as well. Then, after washing her face and brushing her teeth, she crawled between the covers.

An eerie wind wailed at the window like a lost spirit's cries as Savannah tossed and turned, trying to dismiss the unsettling encounter with Blake Winters from her mind.

It wasn't easy. Try as she might, she couldn't forget those mind-blinding kisses, she couldn't deny how right she'd felt in his arms. Rolling over onto her stomach, she pulled the pillow over her head and cursed softly. When would she learn?

She'd already allowed her emotions to rule her head once. With Jerry. And look how disastrous that affair had turned out to be. This attraction to Blake Winters might be unavoidable—after all, he was, in his own way, a fatally attractive man—but it wasn't safe.

And safe was what Savannah was looking for. Because having already made one near-deadly mistake, she wasn't about to let herself make another.

Finally, exhaustion overcame nervousness and Savannah drifted off into a restless sleep, filled with dreams of a demonically handsome, black-caped Dracula sinking his sharp fangs into the neck of an eagerly willing female victim. Whenever the moonlight slashed across his face, the vampire's features bore a disturbing resemblance to those of Blake Winters.

A GLANCE AT HIS WATCH told Blake that it was three hours past midnight. Outside, the storm continued to rage. Inside, the house was quiet, except for the usual creaks and the occasional sound of a branch against a window. He might have been alone. But he wasn't. As he paced the floor of the tower room, Blake was all too aware of the woman on the floor below. A woman he found frighteningly fascinating.

He'd spent the past lonely hours attempting to reassure himself that his feelings for Savannah Starr were nothing to worry about. She was, after all, a remarkably beautiful woman. Any man not attracted to her would have to be blind, dead, or gay. And he was definitely none of those.

Even the fact that he'd experienced such a driving physical need was not so surprising, considering that he'd been without a woman for a very long time. Coming from a broken family, Blake had taken his marriage vows more seriously than many of his Hollywood contemporaries. This rock-solid belief in fidelity had kept him from straying—even when he began to realize that Pamela didn't share what she blatantly dismissed as his outdated, hopelessly naive views concerning marital monogamy.

Perhaps he had been naive, Blake considered—not for the first time since she had thrown the accusation in his face. After all, he'd never had much firsthand experience with love or affection. His father had taken off before he was born; his mother had been an alcoholic who'd tended to forget she had a kid whenever she drank—which was most of the time.

When he was fourteen years old, Blake left his ramshackle mobile home to bum around the oil fields of West Texas. He worked as a roustabout by day, earning twice as much money with a pool cue in the cowboy bars at night. Eschewing sleep for days at a time, between jobs he wrote screenplays that never made it past the studio secretaries—until he came up with a radically new concept for a television cop show.

Although the critics had unanimously raved about *Police Beat*, the television-viewing public, accustomed to car chases and blazing shoot-outs in police shows, had found its stark, cinema-verité look and gritty realism unappealing. Citing dismal ratings, the network had reluctantly canceled the show after the first season.

Despite the cancellation, Blake found that the controversy created by *Police Beat* had generated a great deal of interest. Studio executives who'd refused to answer his phone calls or respond to his query letters began battling each other with the ferocity of pit bulls to sign him to long-term contracts. Having played enough poker to know when he was holding all the aces, Blake decided to make the jump to the big screen.

Although it grated now to think back on it, for a time he'd behaved like the proverbial kid in a candy store. Although he'd certainly never lacked for female companionship, after he was touted in *Variety* as a major player in the industry, there were more stunningly beautiful women than he could count, all dying to go to bed with him. It didn't take long for Blake to realize that they weren't really interested in him at all; it was Hollywood's new wunderkind they wanted to sleep with.

Since such a revelation was not at all flattering to his self-esteem, Blake had vowed never to date another actress. Despite daily temptations, he'd stuck to that vow for three years. Then he'd met Pamela. The stunning blond starlet had auditioned for a role in one of his films, and although she hadn't gotten the part, in her own way she had proved to be single-minded about Blake Winters.

Unlike all the other egocentric actresses he'd known in the past—women who couldn't stop talking about themselves, women whose entire goal in life was fame and fortune—Pamela quickly made Blake the center of her life. She lavished attention on him. She wept when she learned about his checkered youth and tearfully promised that she'd spend the rest of her life making up for his unhappy past. Insisting that she wanted nothing more than to please him, she even professed herself willing to give up her career.

And please Blake she did. In bed and out. But especially in. Her seduction attempts had been about a subtle as a sledgehammer. But they'd worked. Oh, how they'd worked!

It was only later, after they'd married, that Blake learned what a superb actress Pamela actually was—and that the gleaming marble pedestal she had pretended to put him on was made of common, crumbling clay.

After the divorce, which had been messy even by Tinseltown standards, the idea of getting involved with another actress was about as appealing as walking stark-naked into a roomful of killer bees. Instead, he'd thrown himself into a new project, expunging any errant sexual needs with long hours and hard work. Such steadfast diversion had worked—until he'd screened Savannah Starr's last film.

Deep-seated feelings he'd thought had died with his ill-fated marriage had stirred; but with a steely self-control that had always served him well, Blake reminded himself that experiencing sexual desire was one thing; acting on those feelings, yet another. If he didn't want to make love to the woman, then he wouldn't. It was as simple as that.

Or at least that was what he told himself. And, for a time, he even managed to believe it. Until Savannah Starr had shown up at his door resembling a bewitching siren washed ashore by the storm. And even as he'd struggled against her seductive appeal, every instinct Blake possessed told him that this particular siren was capable of luring him into dark, dangerous waters. Waters that were over his head.

4

THE STORM PASSED. The house was draped in a soft blanket of morning fog when Savannah awoke the next morning, aware of a heavy pressure on her chest. Her eyes flew open, but instead of viewing Blake's dark visage, she found herself staring into the unblinking yellow eyes of the cat, which had settled imperiously on her warm body.

"How did you get in here?" The bedroom door was closed. She was certain she remembered locking it. The cat must have followed her into the room. And, upset as she'd been by Blake's outrageous behavior, she simply mustn't have noticed it.

"Trust the man to have a black cat," she muttered, pushing the animal aside. It shot her a resentful glare before leaping gracefully to the floor. "I suppose a normal everyday tabby would be too much to expect."

She rose, reaching out for the robe draped across the foot of the bed. Initially she'd worn the robe to bed, but finding it too bulky, she'd discarded it sometime in the middle of the night, choosing instead to sleep in the nude. As she tied the sash around her waist, she viewed a familiar overnight case on a nearby wing chair.

Her gratitude toward Blake for making his way back down that muddy road in order to retrieve her clothing was quickly displaced by the knowledge that the man had been in her room, watching her sleep. Naked. Vowing to get this damned audition over with as soon as possible, Savannah marched into the adjoining bathroom.

Although she was furious at Blake Winters for having invaded her privacy, as she stood under the pelting spray of hot water, disjointed memories of her uncomfortably sensual dreams flashed through her mind like flickering scenes from the late, late show.

She'd dreamed that she was a young gentlewoman from Boston at the turn of the century, embarked on a once-in-a-lifetime Grand Tour of the Continent. She'd been in England, inexplicably sleeping atop a high feather bed in the Tower of London. Outside, an electrical storm had raged, filling the air with crackling yellow energy.

She'd been awakened by a sudden flash of lightning, followed by a crash of thunder that shook the tower. Gale-force winds flung open the wooden shutters and in the sulphurous glow of light she viewed a bat, perched on the gray stone window ledge.

She opened her mouth to scream, but it was so dry, all she could manage was a faint, ragged gasp. The bat, flapping his gleaming ebony wings, entered the room, landing on her pillow. Frozen with fright, Savannah had stared, transfixed, as the night mammal slowly metamorphosed into a man, clad solely in black.

His face, illuminated by the lightning, was chiseled into planes and shadows, his jet hair swept back from a deep widow's peak. His mouth was sculpted like a poet's, but it was his eyes that captured her attention.

They were bottomless pools. Try as she might, she couldn't look away.

"I've been waiting for you," he said in a low, husky voice that rumbled like distant thunder.

In that suspended moment, Savannah knew that what was to come was inevitable. "Yes," she whispered.

His smile was a flash of white teeth. "You are so incredibly lovely," he murmured, running his hand down the side on her face. A face that, in her dream, remained blessedly unscarred. "And you're mine. All mine."

When those long fingers began to rhythmically stroke her neck, Savannah sighed and closed her eyes.

But he wouldn't allow her to succumb so easily. "I want to hear you say it." When his thumb lingered on the pulse at the base of her throat, Savannah knew he could feel the rapid beat of her heart. "Open your eyes and tell me that you belong to me."

As if by their own volition, her lashes fluttered open and Savannah found herself once again trapped by his glowing gaze. "Yours," she managed through lips that had gone unbearably dry. "Only yours."

"For eternity."

"For eternity," she echoed dreamily.

Satisfied, he flashed her another brilliant smile. And then slowly, inexorably, he lowered his dark head.

Savannah experienced an initial flash of exquisite pain when his teeth settled into the vulnerable skin of her neck. As he supped unhurriedly, she felt a warm, steady pull between her legs, an ache that grew more intense the longer he drank from her flesh.

Passion rose. Thunder and lightning coursed through her, and just when she thought she'd faint from ecstasy, the storm broke and she lay trembling in his arms, totally possessed.

SAVANNAH HAD NEVER believed in dreams as omens, but there was something undeniably intriguing about this one. . . .

"No!" Frustrated, she began scrubbing the floral-scented shampoo into her hair. It was only a nightmare, brought on by the storm, her strange surroundings, and the traumatic experience of trudging through the wind and rain and lightning to this Gothic monstrosity of a house.

That was all it was, she told herself furiously. That was all she would allow it to be.

But when she entered the kitchen twenty minutes later and viewed Blake's unnerving resemblance to the darkly seductive vampire in her dream, a frisson of fear, mingled with remembered passion, skimmed up Savannah's spine.

Frustrated by his uncharacteristic emotionalism, Blake told himself that he had no intention of getting involved with Savannah Starr. All he wanted from her was a score for his film. Nothing more.

He'd almost managed to convince himself of that when the woman who'd caused him such unwanted turmoil entered the kitchen looking like a wood nymph in olive-green corduroy slacks and a matching sweater.

Blake frowned. "Good morning," he greeted her with a distinct lack of enthusiasm that hid the automatic sexual response her appearance created.

"Good morning."

Savannah had hoped that in the bright light of day, Blake Winters would appear less forbidding. But as she watched that all-too-familiar scowl carve its way across his granite-like features, she realized that the man was every bit as cold and disagreeable as he'd seemed the night before.

His gaze was inscrutable as he handed her a glass of juice. "I didn't expect to see you up this early."

Although Savannah had always considered herself an honest person, she decided against admitting that sexual dreams starring her host had shaken her from a restless sleep. "The sooner we get started, the sooner I can leave," she said instead.

She took a sip of the juice. It tasted like nectar. Even living in the land of citrus groves, Savannah couldn't remember the last time she'd been treated to fresh orange juice. "This is delicious."

"When I was a kid growing up in the West Texas oil patch, I had the mistaken idea that everyone in California had fresh orange juice every morning."

"Which they laced with vintage champagne. While sitting beside their Beverly Hills pools," Savannah added. The cat, which had followed her downstairs, twined sensually between her ankles. "Surrounded by tropical flowers."

"Roses," he corrected with a rare smile. "Acres and acres of American Beauty roses. All the women would be blond and beautiful and the men, tanned and powerful."

Savannah found herself responding to the warmth of his smile. "And they all made megabuck movie deals before breakfast."

"That's about it," he agreed. "When I grew up and discovered that things weren't exactly the way the movies had made them out to be, I decided that squeezing a few oranges every morning was as close as I'd ever get to the fantasy."

"But you've certainly succeeded beyond fresh orange juice," she said. "After all, along with making quite a few megabuck deals yourself, you've lived in Beverly Hills—"

"My wife lived there," he corrected brusquely. "I hated the place."

Well, Savannah decided with an inner sigh, the easygoing conversation had been nice while it lasted. Unfortunately, the gruff, unsociable Blake Winters was back. In spades.

"My point was that you've achieved amazing success," she insisted quietly. "Wasn't it a columnist for the *Hollywood Reporter* who described you as 'the quintessential self-made man'?"

His eyebrows drew together in a forbidding line as his scowl deepened. "You are the last person I would have expected to believe everything you read."

Savannah knew he was referring to the way her life, as well as that of her parents, had always provided grist for the press gossip-mill. She'd learned at an early age that when her activities failed to provide titillating copy, the more unscrupulous reporters would simply make up a scandalous story to sell papers. Readers, apparently, didn't care whether or not the story was true, so long as it lived up to their expectations of sin-drenched Hollywood Personalities.

She met his disapproving gaze with a long, level look of her own. "I don't."

Something passed between them. Something as potent as it was fleeting. Something that Blake knew he'd have to think about—later, when he was alone.

"Well," he said, pouring coffee into a pair of hand-crafted earthenware mugs, "the rags certainly didn't lie when they said you were even more beautiful in person than you appear on the screen."

Savannah was disappointed by the way he'd stooped to false flattery. Last night, Blake Winters may not have been very warm or gracious, but at least he'd seemed different from the run-of-the-mill Hollywood wolf. Apparently she'd been wrong.

"That's very kind of you to say," she said stiffly. "But you don't have to lie. I know what I look like. I face my scars every time I look in the mirror."

In an effort to dissuade any ideas Blake might have for continuing where they had left off last night, Savannah had purposely pulled her thick hair back from her face. Other than a light application of pale pink gloss on her lips, she had forgone makeup. Although she was loath to admit it, she realized that her actions had been a test to see if he would still want her after viewing her scars in the unforgiving morning sunlight.

"Don't be so hypersensitive." He waved away her words with an impatient flick of his wrist. "I couldn't see them at all last night, in the candlelight. Even by daylight, they're barely visible. Certainly those few faint lines aren't enough to keep you from resuming your acting career."

Even as she was surprised by Blake's easy acceptance of her disfigurement, Savannah refused to consider such a proposal. To her, the scars had achieved daunting proportions, scarring her self-esteem as well as her face. "I'm not returning to the screen."

He gave her a long, searching look that made Savannah feel he could see all the way to her soul. "Suit yourself. I, for one, am damned glad you decided to turn your creative energies toward your music."

Savannah was relieved at the mention of the professional reason for her being here. The conversation had been getting uncomfortably personal. "About the score—"

"After breakfast."

"That's right," she muttered. "You don't believe in doing business when you're eating." She looked at him curiously. "I can't see you in Hollywood at all," she said, thinking how mealtimes were more often than not just another opportunity for deal making.

"Neither could I," he said. "Which is why I don't live there." He gestured toward the doorway. "I thought we'd have breakfast in the sun-room."

Although Savannah had never been much of a morning eater, she found it impossible to resist the enticing aromas wafting from the oven. She watched in awe as he removed the baking pans and placed them on the ceramic counter. Streusel-topped muffins and golden biscuits lured her.

"How many people do you intend to feed?"

"Just the two of us." He handed her a wooden tray. "You can take the coffee. Oh, and the jam." A dish of ruby-colored preserves joined the coffee carafe and mugs on the tray.

"I don't usually eat jam."

"You'll love this." He overrode her protest. "I made it from huckleberries that grow wild in the woods."

"*People* magazine would probably pay a bundle to know that Hollywood's most reclusive wunderkind makes his own jams and jellies."

"Too boring."

This time the smile reached his eyes—eyes that were the color of the fresh-brewed coffee he'd given her. Savannah stared, momentarily transfixed by their gleaming warmth. To her vast relief, Blake appeared not to notice the effect he'd had on her.

"The sun-room's down the hall, around a couple of corners, third door on the left," he said. "Just stay in the main hallway and you won't get lost. I'll bring the rest of the stuff."

The narrow corridor twisted and turned like a maze. As she walked along it, Savannah tried to memorize the way back to the kitchen. But by the time she reached the plant-filled solarium, she was totally disoriented.

Walking through the doorway was like stepping through a time machine. A quick glance around the room had Savannah deciding that Queen Victoria and Prince Albert would have been at home with the antique black wicker furniture and leafy, dark green foliage.

She was studying the botanical prints on the wall when a strange, almost-human voice called out,

"Nevermore." Spinning around, she saw a large black bird staring at her from his perch in a cage in front of the bay window.

"It's no wonder you made a horror film," she said when Blake joined her. "After living in this place."

He lifted a dark eyebrow. "You don't like my house?"

"The house is okay. More than okay," she admitted. "In its own rather quirky way, it's spectacular. What I'm referring to is the way you've gone overboard to make it so damn spooky."

"If you're taking about Cujo," Blake said blandly, nodding toward the black mynah bird, "he belongs to a magician friend. After he got a gig touring clubs in Canada, Sam discovered he couldn't take his bird with him. Something about animal-health laws. So I agreed to keep Cujo as a favor."

She glanced over at the bird with an unwilling fascination. "What kind of person names his bird *Cujo?*"

After reading the horror tale about a killer dog, Savannah had never felt completely comfortable around Saint Bernards. As if responding to his name, the bird suddenly flapped his wings, left his open cage and came to perch on the back of her chair.

"Congratulations," Blake said. "Cujo doesn't take to many people. As for his name, Sam's a rabid Stephen King fan. He also has a sense of the bizarre."

Remembering the novel in graphic detail, Savannah wished that Blake had chosen some other term besides *rabid*. She cast a cautionary glance upward at the mynah bird, who stared back at her with bright, shoe-button eyes.

"Good night, sweet prince," Cujo cackled.

"A bird named after a dog in a Stephen King novel who quotes Shakespeare and Poe," Savannah mused. "Fascinating."

"Sam used to be a high-school English teacher," Blake explained easily. "I figure that Cujo picked up a lot of stuff hanging around the classroom."

Savannah looked over at the cat, who had curled up under a slender beam of pale yellow sunlight.

"I suppose that explains Cujo," she said. "What about the black cat? I'm almost afraid to ask his name."

Blake shrugged. "I've never known it, although he answers to Cat. When he wants to answer, that is. He showed up one night in the middle of a storm, wet, bedraggled and demanding food. Once fed, he refused to leave."

Although Savannah tried to tell herself that a man who'd rescue a stranded cat in a thunderstorm couldn't be all that bad, she still couldn't quite relax in Blake Winters's presence.

Thirty minutes later, Savannah was staring at her empty plate in disbelief. "I can't believe I ate all that."

The biscuits had been delicious, flaky and buttery. The homemade huckleberry jam had been everything Blake had promised; it tasted like ambrosia. As for the muffins . . . *Betty Crocker, eat your heart out.*

"You could stand to gain a few pounds," Blake said as he refilled their coffee cups. "You're too thin."

"A woman can never be too rich or too thin," Savannah answered automatically. The Duchess of Windsor's famous words were one of Savannah's earliest memories of her mother, who had quoted them continually.

"Men prefer curves," he argued. "Something to hold on to in bed."

Like his wife? Savannah wondered. Pamela Winters certainly wasn't lacking in the curve department. Savannah sipped her coffee, pretending indifference. The same way she pretended that she hadn't noticed the stimulating contrast between the feminine lines of Blake's black wicker armchair and the man's innate masculinity.

"You realize, of course," she said archly, "that is an incredibly chauvinistic statement."

"Perhaps. It's also true."

"Well, since we're never going to bed together, I don't see that my weight is any of your business."

He shrugged again in that frustratingly masculine gesture of nonchalance that Savannah was beginning to hate. "Never say never," he advised. Before Savannah could insist that she had no intention of having an affair with him, Blake proved yet again that he was a master of manipulation.

"How would you like to see the final cut of *Unholy Matrimony?*"

Knowing his penchant for secrecy, Savannah was surprised by the unexpected offer. "It depends. Do I have to sign a pledge of secrecy in blood?"

Something resembling a smile flickered across Blake's lips. "That depends on whether or not I can trust you."

Despite his casual tone, something in his eyes told Savannah that they were suddenly talking about a great deal more than her willingness to keep his script a secret.

"I suppose you'll have to be the judge of that." Although her voice was steady, her nerves were not as he gave her another of those long, probing looks.

"Out, damned spot!" Cujo croaked. Neither Blake nor Savannah appeared to take notice.

After what seemed an eternity, Blake appeared to have made up his mind. "It runs nearly three hours," he warned her.

Savannah wondered if the studio executives knew that, and decided they didn't. And although watching such a lengthy film would use up valuable time that she should be using to score her scenes—she still couldn't believe she'd actually agreed to audition!—Savannah couldn't resist the opportunity to be the first person to see the story in its entirety.

"I'm not doing anything important at the moment," she said.

With the air of a man accustomed to getting his way, Blake appeared to have expected no other answer. "Fine. I've already set up the projector. We'll talk about the scoring later."

When she stood, Cujo left the back of her chair with a loud flutter of wings, and settled on her shoulder. She froze.

"Amazing," Blake murmured. With the merest flick of his wrist, he coaxed the bird from Savannah's shoulder to his arm. "Sorry, old boy," he said as he transferred the mynah bird into his cage. "But it's time for work. You can visit with Ms. Starr later."

"Come up and see me sometime," the bird answered obligingly.

SAVANNAH FOLLOWED Blake down the Byzantine hallway to his private screening room. The room, decorated for the comfort of its owner, reminded her of an English gentlemen's club: lots of dark wood and oversize furniture. Turning down his offer of more coffee, she settled into a bark-brown leather chair, prepared to watch the film with him. But the titles had no sooner flashed on the screen when Blake turned to leave the room.

"Aren't you going to watch?" she asked.

"I've seen it. Besides, you'll have a more honest reaction if you can watch it without worrying about me watching your every reaction. I'll be down on the beach when you're done. I left a slicker and boots for you in the foyer."

He had a point, Savannah decided. A point that was driven home even harder as she sat alone in the dark and watched Blake's lengthy black comedy unfold on the screen. The rumors about his film being a thinly disguised story of his own marriage were obviously true.

It was bad enough that the voluptuous blond actress playing the deadly female vampire could have been Pamela Winters's double. Even more damning was the fact that the woman had all Pamela's gestures down pat—even the way she had of licking her lips whenever she was about to take advantage of her husband. That same seductive look had been captured by the photographer who shot Pamela's *Playboy* layout.

Savannah had seen that gorgeous face smiling out from the cover of the magazine at the newsstand just last week. Stories of Pamela Winters's body being the product of several sessions with a Brazilian plastic surgeon had circulated around Hollywood for years. When she'd viewed that famous figure, seductively posed and scantily clad in a gold lamé bikini the size of a Band-Aid strip, Savannah had decided that if the rumors of surgical body-sculpting were even remotely true, Blake's former wife had definitely gotten her money's worth.

As the story continued to unfold, Savannah found herself both transfixed and appalled by Blake's savagely critical view of marriage. Some of the scenes were so scathingly misogynistic, she couldn't help wondering if it was only his ex-wife Blake hated—or if his distaste for women was all-encompassing. Even as she told herself that she wasn't the least bit interested in the man, Savannah found the idea that Blake would put her in the same category with Pamela strangely depressing.

UNABLE TO REMAIN passive while Savannah watched the final cut of *Unholy Matrimony,* Blake strode along the beach, furious to find himself anxious for her approval. He'd already fallen for one woman's seductive schemes; he wasn't about to repeat the experience. What he should do, Blake decided, was simply tell her that she wasn't right for the job and send her packing.

Savannah Starr wasn't the only musician in Hollywood. Unfortunately, he reminded himself grimly, she was the only one he wanted.

BY THE TIME the final credits rolled onto the screen, it had begun to sprinkle again. She located the hooded slicker and was surprised to find that it fit perfectly. So did the boots. More proof that he had been expecting her.

Excited about the prospect of scoring his film, Savannah was not as annoyed as she once might have been by Blake's arrogant assumption that she wouldn't be able to turn down an opportunity to audition for him.

The beach was a far cry from the sun-warmed silver sand at her Malibu home. Instead of delicate pink and ivory seashells, rocks lined the stretch of sand between the surf and the jagged cliffs. Jellyfish, the size of marbles, shimmered on the wet sand between the rocks; tiny crabs edged sideways back to the sea. Along with the jellyfish and crabs, the ebbing tide had left behind an amazing amount of kelp. It covered everything, like a thick, green net left behind by a careless fisherman.

She found him in a moderately sheltered cove about a quarter mile from the house. He was sitting on a rock beside a tide pool.

"Look at this," he said, forgoing a more conventional greeting. He'd seen her coming; in the shiny yellow slicker and matching boots, she'd stood out in the gray mist like the warmth of a sunbeam. Just the sight of her had made him want to smile. Irritated by the way she caused his emotions to careen out of control, he'd resisted the urge.

Savannah looked.

"It's oil," he told her unnecessarily. "Damn, I get angry about the way we're treating this planet."

Personally, Savannah had come to the conclusion that Blake Winters got angry about almost everything;

but she decided, for the sake of peace and future employment, to keep her thoughts to herself.

"Is that why you made that environmental short the Sierra Club showed to Congress last week?"

He shot her a dangerous look. "How did you know about that? I insisted that my name not be associated with the project in any way."

"I'm a member of Malibu's Save Our Beaches committee. We rented the film to use as a fund-raiser a few months ago. I thought at the time the camera work seemed familiar. The minute I saw the woods scene in *Unholy Matrimony*, I recognized the location." She looked at him curiously. "The work is brilliant. I can't understand why you'd want to remain anonymous."

"I've never approved of Hollywood types using their fame to promote a cause," he said. "But that doesn't mean that I don't have some very strong views. Making the film anonymously ensured that the message, not me, would be the story."

"That makes sense," she decided. "But I hope you realize that you're not going to be able to avoid comparisons between *Unholy Matrimony* and your own life," she said carefully.

After having witnessed how autobiographical his film was, Savannah felt as if she were walking on eggshells. But she also realized that she'd been given valuable insight into this frustratingly closed, intensely private man.

To Savannah's amazement, Blake threw back his head and laughed. Stunned by his unexpected behavior, she found herself drawn to the rich, deep sound.

"Pamela's already filed a lawsuit," he told her when he'd stopped laughing.

"But that will only bring the picture more publicity."

"I know. But my former wife's IQ was always a smaller number than her cup size."

"That's not a very flattering thing to say," the feminist in Savannah felt obliged to point out.

"It's not nearly as bad as the stuff she told the press about me."

Including letting everyone believe her husband had tried to kill her. "You may have a point," Savannah said quietly. "May I ask a question?"

"I suppose that depends on the question."

"Do you dislike *all* women? Or only actresses?"

His stony jaw clenched. "I don't know what you're talking about."

"Don't you? If *Unholy Matrimony* is any example of your feelings—"

"Now you're acting as paranoid as my ex-wife," he said tightly. "I've already stated on record, to Pamela's attorneys, that my film is not autobiographical."

Having seen the film in question, Savannah wasn't deterred that easily. If they were to work together, she intended to make certain that she wasn't going to be lumped into the same unpleasant category as Blake's egocentric, self-indulgent former spouse.

"Please don't dodge the issue," she insisted quietly. "This is important to me."

Something in the level way she met his gaze moved Blake. He tried to remind himself that women were masters of guile. And even if he wanted to believe that Savannah was an anomaly—an honest woman—all he had to do was take a cold, hard look at his own scars to remind himself exactly how calculating the female of the species could be. She was, after all—like Pamela—an actress. And a damn good one.

"I don't discuss my personal life. The only two things you need to know are that I honestly admire your talent, and that rumors of my trying to kill my former wife are not true." He smiled. It was a grim, challenging smile that held no humor. "So, you can relax. Your life won't be in danger while you're working with me."

Despite the chill in the air, warmth suffused her cheeks. Savannah was so embarrassed that she didn't protest his use of the word *while* instead of if in discussing the possibility of their working together. "I wasn't—"

"Of course you were," Blake countered without rancor. "Everyone who read those damn accusations was bound to wonder if they were true. Even I have to admit that the story has a rather tawdry fascination about it—maverick Hollywood screenwriter weds beautiful, ambitious, well-endowed starlet, only to discover that she's got the morals of an alley cat.

"If that weren't bad enough, when he discovers the fatal truth that she only married him for what he could do for her career, his male ego—which has been hanging by a thread due to her infidelities—is shattered. The knowledge eats away at him, day after day, like poison, until he finally seeks revenge by cutting her brake lines." He shrugged. "It happens all the time."

The rain was slanting harder now, but it was the latent bitterness in Blake's voice that chilled Savannah to the bone.

"In the movies," she murmured.

His sharp eyes didn't miss her slight shiver. "In the movies," he agreed. The conversation was getting too personal. What was it about this woman that made him want to spill his guts? He'd always been an extremely private person. Life was better than way. Safer.

"It's getting cold," he said, changing the subject. "Let's go back to the house and you can tell me what you think about the film."

As they walked back up the beach together, Savannah decided that she wasn't the only one who'd been severely scarred by a disastrous choice in lovers. The only difference between her and Blake was that her scars were more visible.

5

ALTHOUGH BLAKE HAD assured Savannah in his letter that he had all the equipment she needed to score the scenes, she wasn't expecting the fully outfitted studio he'd set up. Unlike the rest of the house, this room was starkly utilitarian.

The synthesizer—that electronic marvel that had all but murdered a once-thriving Los Angeles studio-music scene—was state-of-the-art. As was the computer that would allow her to match the music to picture-to-picture cuts with a computerized time code.

A large-screen television with a patented flat picture-tube for improved visual quality stood in the corner of the room; a dual-track VCR sat on a nearby shelf.

"Well," Savannah said as she stared around the amazingly outfitted studio in wonder, "no one can accuse you of not being prepared."

"You can't achieve perfection without the proper tools."

Savannah decided that it would save them both time if she was honest. "If you're looking for perfection, you definitely have the wrong person."

He gave her another of those long, judicious looks. "I don't think so."

"But—"

"Don't worry. I don't expect *absolute* perfection."
Before she could respond, he said, "*Ordinary* perfection will be quite sufficient."

For a moment Savannah believed him to be serious.
Then he smiled, in an abruptly charming way.

A ripple of anxiety made Savannah realize that Blake
Winters's smiles were even more dangerous than his
scowls. Reminding herself that the man represented a
pitfall she had every intention of avoiding, Savannah
refused to turn to putty just because Blake had decided
that she'd make a good bedmate.

"Then we have nothing to worry about," she said.
Her gaze was level and challenged the invitation in his.
"From the marvelous scenes you've given me to work
with, ordinary perfection should be no problem at all."

Having long ago decided that one learned more from
faces than words, Blake watched the range of emotions cross Savannah's face: reluctant desire, anxiety,
determination.

"I suppose we should get down to work, then.
There's a video of the scenes I'd like you to score in the
VCR. Would you mind if I stayed and watched you
work?"

Savannah was surprised by the question. She would
have bet her Oscar that Blake wasn't a man accustomed to seeking permission for anything from anyone.

"It's your studio."

She sat down at the synthesizer, turned on the computer and the VCR. Then she switched on the television and watched the first scene of the two she was to
score come onto the screen.

As Blake watched Savannah work, he decided that he'd never seen such concentration. Of course she hadn't minded him staying in the studio; as far as she was concerned, she was all alone in the room.

Lost in her work the way she was, it crossed his mind that the house could be on fire and she wouldn't notice. Instead, every atom of her attention was directed toward the television screen and synthesizer.

She was working on the scene where the protagonist discovered his wife to be a vampire. Although Blake would never claim musical talent, he suspected that most musicians would have chosen a thunderous, dramatic sound, lots of brass and drums. And they would have been wrong.

Blake listened, intrigued by Savannah's intuitive sense. It was as if she'd tapped into his mind—as well as his heart—allowing her to know exactly what he'd been thinking.

The music she'd chosen was the cool, lonely melody of an alto sax. A sound that reminded Blake exactly how coldly furious he'd been, how betrayed he'd felt, when he discovered that Pamela had only married him for what he could do for her.

A perfectionist himself, Blake wasn't surprised to find that Savannah shared that character trait. Even when he thought she'd hit exactly the right note, she continued to rework certain phrases, rearrange a bridge here and there, change a segment from major to minor key.

By the time she was satisfied with the scene, it was late. When she finally returned to the real world, Savannah was surprised to see that the sky outside the arched window was growing dark. It was always like this when she worked; time ceased to exist.

"I'd better be going."

"You've only scored one scene. You still have another one to do."

"I'll stay at the inn down the road and come back in the morning."

"It's been raining off and on all day," Blake reminded her. "That road will be like quicksand. Besides, we haven't worked out the terms of our contract."

"Contracts are for agents," Savannah countered. But as she looked out the window again and watched the fog settle around the house, the idea of navigating that treacherous road again in the dark was decidedly unappealing. "But I guess you're right about the road. I suppose I don't have any choice but to spend one more night."

"I knew you were an intelligent woman," he said. "As well as an extremely talented one. What you did with that scene was absolutely brilliant."

His compliment shouldn't make her feel so good. It shouldn't warm her all over. But, heaven help her, it did. "Thank you."

"In a way, it was spooky. Like you were somehow inside my head."

She smiled. "Nothing that paranormal. I simply thought about how it felt to be betrayed by the person you thought you knew. And loved."

They exchanged a long look. "I think," Blake said finally, "that this is going to be a very interesting collaboration."

Her heart skipped a beat. "Are you saying I've got the job?"

"If you want it."

Savannah resisted the urge to fling her arms around his neck. Instead she gave him a dazzling smile. "You've got yourself a musician."

It was what he'd wanted from the beginning. But now that he had Savannah Starr, Blake found himself wondering what the hell he was going to do with her.

DINNER WAS A ROBUST fisherman's stew, a Western Caesar salad that exchanged crumbly blue cheese for the anchovies, and crunchy sourdough bread. Savannah was relieved when Blake admitted that he'd bought the bread from a San Francisco bakery. His skill in the kitchen, compared to her own scant culinary talents, was vaguely intimidating. It would have been too much to discover that he'd kneaded the bread dough with those strong, capable hands.

After dinner, they went upstairs to the tower room. Going over to the stone fireplace, Blake lit the fire he'd set that morning. The kindling caught and a warm, crackling glow began to dispel the night chill in the air. It was raining again; a shimmering curtain of water washed down the windowpanes. Thick fog gradually obscured the sliver of silver moon.

A not-uncomfortable silence settled over them as they sat on the leather sofa, both seeming content to stare into the flickering orange-and-blue flames as they listened to the steady *tap, tap, tap* of rain against the glass. Cujo, who'd been brought upstairs from the sun-room, remained silent as he sat on his perch and groomed his gleaming black feathers. The cat, not waiting for an invitation, climbed into Savannah's lap. It was Blake who finally broke the silence.

"I suppose, if we're going to work together, we need to talk about it," he said. "About Pamela's accident. And all those rumors that her brush with death wasn't accidental, that I'd arranged for the brakes to fail on her car after I'd found her with a lover."

It wasn't his first choice. Blake was surprised to realize that what he really wanted was to simply sit here with her and enjoy the fire and talk about anything that wasn't important. But although he'd told himself that he didn't give a damn whether people believed the stories about him trying to kill his ex-wife, it was suddenly very important that Savannah knew the truth.

Savannah had her own reasons for fearing an obsessively jealous man. But she couldn't believe Blake would be capable of such a heinous crime, and she told him so.

"There was a time when I wished her dead," Blake revealed quietly. He wasn't looking at Savannah. Instead he was staring at the flames. From the grim line of his jaw, Savannah guessed that he was recalling a particularly unpleasant moment in his ill-fated marriage. "But I never would have done anything about it."

"I know."

He turned toward her. "You sound very sure of that."

It was Savannah's turn to gaze into the fire. As she absently stroked the ebony fur beneath her fingertips, the cat's purr sounded like a small motor in the stillness of the room.

"I've had firsthand experience with a murderous man," she reminded him in a voice that was little more than a whisper. "And I know that you're nothing like Jerry Larsen."

Although he was admittedly curious about what kind of man could possibly bring himself to harm any woman, let alone this one, Blake didn't want to pry. After demanding privacy himself, it would be the height of hypocrisy to try to delve into Savannah's painful past.

"You don't have to talk about it," he said.

"It's all right." She didn't take her eyes from the hypnotic flames. "After what you told me about your wife, it seems only fair that I share something equally personal."

She took a deep breath, trying to decide where to start. How could she explain that even having grown up in Hollywood, where children of stars were often exposed at an early age to the harsh realities of life, she'd been naive in ways Blake Winters could never understand.

"Jerry was a struggling impressionist and would-be actor when I met him at a comedy club," she said slowly. Her voice was distant, as if she were lost in her own private reverie. Or nightmare.

"Mutual friends introduced him, and after his show we went out for coffee. He was funny and he made me laugh. Which probably wouldn't have been enough to base a relationship on if my mother hadn't recently committed suicide." She took another deeper, more painfully ragged breath. "I felt so alone."

Blake realized how difficult this was for her. After all, he reminded himself, he'd been able to exorcise his pain by making his film. Savannah, it seemed, was still carrying much of hers inside.

His desire to make love to Savannah warred with a strong, unbidden desire to put his arm around her and offer solace. In the end, he did neither.

"I've got the picture. You don't have to say any more." But he didn't have the entire picture. And even as he heard himself saying otherwise, Blake realized, with some discomfort, that he wanted to know all about Savannah's relationship with the man who had been sent to prison for nearly killing her.

She dragged her eyes from the flames and met his sympathetic gaze. "I think I do," she whispered. She forced a smile that failed. "During all those reconstructive operations, my doctor tried to talk me into seeing a therapist. Apparently it's standard procedure for people who've suffered disfiguring injuries."

"You're hardly disfigured," Blake pointed out. "But I can appreciate the concept. It must be difficult to look in the mirror and see a stranger looking back at you."

"Unbearably difficult," she admitted. "Which is why I refused to look in the mirror for months."

"Months?" He found it difficult to believe. Surely human curiosity would overwhelm any fear a person might be harboring.

"Months," Savannah repeated. "But even after I was able to face my physical scars, I couldn't quite get up the courage to face my emotional ones. So I canceled my appointment with the psychologist." She returned her gaze to the fire.

Tenderness invaded Blake, making him cautious. He felt as if he'd been handed a grenade whose pin had been pulled. Although the way she'd gotten under his skin was irritating the hell out of him, the one thing he didn't want to do was to say or do anything that would cause Savannah additional pain. Because even as he'd fought like hell against feeling anything for her, he was slowly beginning to realize that he just might be fighting a losing battle.

Savannah was relieved when Blake remained silent, allowing her to collect her thoughts and muster up her nerve. A log collapsed, sending a brilliant flare of sparks into the air. Unable to sit still, she pushed the cat off her lap, rose to her feet, walked over to the fireplace and began jabbing restlessly at the fragrant cedar logs with the poker.

"In the beginning, Jerry was amazingly attentive. It was as if he'd put me on top of a high pedestal and, to tell the truth, for a time I rather enjoyed the view."

Her lips drew into a faint sad smile that failed to touch her eyes. "My parents weren't around much when I was growing up. I spent most of my time with housekeepers, or away at school. Jerry was the first person, other than Justin, who treated me as if I were someone special."

"I've been there," Blake said grimly.

Savannah turned and looked directly at Blake. His face was as inscrutable as ever, but she thought she could see something in his eyes. Empathy? Sympathy? Or worse yet, pity? Unwilling to consider that unpalatable thought, she continued her story.

"After we started dating, Jerry began to distance me from my friends. It was a gradual thing. He kept telling me that he loved me so much that he couldn't bear to share me with anyone."

Her fingers curved around the poker in a death grip; her knuckles were white. "Looking back, I realize that I should have realized what was happening, but at the time, it seemed so wonderful—being the most important thing in his life."

What she didn't say was that after a lifetime of careless attention from her famous parents, Jerry's possessiveness had seemed the answer to all her youthful prayers. Eventually, she realized that Jerry was not at all the man she'd thought him to be. The warm, loving, attentive Jerry was merely a fantasy, born of her lonely need.

Blake, remembering how he'd fallen for Pamela's clever pretense, could certainly identify with that. "Did you love him?" he heard himself ask.

"I thought I did," Savannah said on a soft sigh. "In the beginning. Now I realize I was only in love with the idea of being in love." She combed her hand through her hair in an unconscious gesture that made it settle around her face in an ebony cloud.

"But then things changed. After I let Jerry move into my house, it was as if he'd lost interest. He started disappearing for days at a time. And when he'd return, there would be signs of another woman. His sweater would carry a scent I'd never worn, there'd be lipstick a color other than mine on his shirt collar, little slips of papers with phone numbers written on them began appearing on the bureau."

"Why did you put up with all that?" Blake asked. "Why did you stay?"

"I don't know." Savannah rubbed her ice-cold arms and tried to come up with the answer that had successfully evaded her for months. "If anyone had told me that I'd become so dependent on anyone—especially a man who treated me horribly—I would have laughed. No," she decided with a burst of heated emotion, "I would have been furious. But for some reason I still can't comprehend, once I found myself in that situation, I couldn't see things clearly."

She drew in a deep, ragged breath. "I realize now that I should have been furious, but in the beginning, all I could do was wonder what I'd done wrong to cause Jerry to have those affairs."

"I know the feeling," Blake said. "Very well."

For a fleeting moment his mask fell, and Savannah knew that he understood.

"Even when his behavior got worse, I didn't leave. Up here I knew I was behaving like an idiot—" she touched a shaky finger to her temple "—but I couldn't make myself leave. Even today, it makes no sense."

Lingering feelings of self-contempt intensified the pounding behind her eyes. "Gradually, I began to suspect that he was only with me to further his own career. I'd already opened a lot of doors for him— Letterman, *The Tonight Show*. Although Justin never liked Jerry, he agreed to pull some strings and get him included in an HBO special on rising young comics."

"I saw that show," Blake remembered. "The guy's not half bad."

"He's very talented," Savannah agreed. "He was also in a hurry to reach the top. Anyway, he was up for a part in a made-for-television movie—it was a pilot for a planned series—when he leaked the news to the press that he and I were getting married. Fortunately, one of the few friends I had left had been signed to direct the film. She told me that Jerry had promised the network that if they gave him the part, I'd agree to co-star."

"Which would guarantee ratings."

"Exactly. He knew that I was scheduled to do a film of my own at the same time, but I suppose he figured that I'd be willing to sacrifice my own career for his. After all, I'd given him control over far more personal aspects of my life."

She frowned and poked at the log again, causing another shower of sparks. "But what was even worse, he told the network executives that I'd also agreed to do the series. For scale. So long as he was cast in the leading role. When I asked him about it, he didn't even bother to lie.

"When I told him to get out, he hit me. Hard, right in here, with his fist." She pressed her hand against her stomach. "No one had ever hit me before and I was amazed at how much it hurt. I tried to get away, but he kept hitting me, again and again, holding me up so I couldn't fall. All the time he kept telling me the only reason he was with me—the only reason anyone would stay with me—was because of what I could do for his career."

"Why the hell didn't you call the police after he assaulted you?"

"There'd already been so much publicity about my mother's suicide, I couldn't face the prospect of my personal problems being spread all over the tabloids. I hated the idea of people all over the world knowing the most painful aspects of my private life.

"And," she admitted haltingly, "I was so ashamed. All I wanted was to be free of Jerry, to get my life back on track."

Blake, who'd never been the slightest bit interested in Hollywood gossip, was surprised at how clearly he recalled that day. He'd been watching the evening news when, at a commercial break, a promo for *Entertainment Tonight* had come on. Savannah Starr's walking out on the man who'd been accused by many Hollywood insiders of manipulating her career for his own gain, was scheduled to be that night's *Inside Story*. Knowing firsthand how it felt to be used by someone trying to further a career, Blake had felt a certain empathy for Savannah.

"That's when you called the affair off."

"Yes." She shook her head at the memory of what followed. "But instead of freeing myself, all I succeeded in doing was turning Jerry's jealousy into an obsession."

Her bottom lip trembled, her complexion was dead white, her eyes wide and dark. Her soft voice was thready with remembered horror. "He kept telephoning, screaming obscenities at me. I changed unlisted phone numbers three times, which would earn me a few days' peace. But every time, he somehow managed to learn the new number and the calls began again." She was staring off into the distance, deep in her own painful memories.

"I assume you went to the police."

She dug her nails into her palms. Even now, after all these months, just talking about her accident could cause fear to bubble in her veins.

"Of course," she managed through lips that had gone unbearably dry. "And a very nice detective explained that although it was unfortunate, there wasn't much they could do until Jerry actually tried to hurt me."

The story was eerily familiar to Blake. He'd written a similar plotline for *Police Beat*. The episode revolving around an insanely jealous banker who brutally murdered his estranged wife had earned Blake an Emmy.

Savannah touched the scar bisecting her cheek distractedly. When Blake saw her hand tremble, he experienced a sudden urge to curse the man who caused her such agony. But, not wanting to interrupt, he held his tongue.

"After he started spending the night in his car outside my house, I went to court and got a restraining order."

"Which doesn't do a damn thing."

"It didn't in my case," Savannah agreed grimly.

She squeezed her eyes tightly shut and pressed the heels of her hands against them, as if to block out the still-vivid images that had haunted her nightly when she first left the hospital. Savannah considered the fact that she now only had the nightmares once or twice a week to be an improvement.

"One of the nurses told me that I was still holding the paper when the ambulance brought me to the hospital."

Rage came swiftly, steamrolling over sympathy. A burst of primal passion he hadn't felt since his days in the oil patch made Blake want to kill the bastard who'd done such a job, both physically and emotionally, on Savannah.

She sighed. A long, weary sigh fraught with regret. "It was about nine o'clock. I'd returned home after having dinner with Cody Shannon, the actor who'd costarred with me in *Seduced*.

"The film had finished shooting that day and we'd gone out to celebrate after the wrap party, which was probably a mistake since the fan magazines were reporting that we'd had a hot affair during the filming. They even got their hands on a piece of film of our lovemaking scene and passed the photos off as real. But our relationship really was strictly platonic. If nothing else, Cody was happily married, and I'd never, in a million years, get involved with a married man."

Blake lifted his hands. "Hey, you don't have to convince me of anything, Savannah. Whether or not you were romantically involved with the guy isn't any of my business. And it damn sure wasn't any of Larsen's."

"It shouldn't have been," she agreed raggedly. "But unfortunately Jerry wasn't the kind of man to let go easily. He'd broken into my house and was waiting for me. I asked him to leave, he refused. We exchanged words, the argument escalated. His accusations grew more and more bizarre."

She began to tremble, despite the warmth of the fire. "Finally, when I tried to call the police, he shoved me. His strength surprised me. It was almost inhuman. Like something from a horror movie . . ."

Fighting for control, Savannah clutched her hands together until her fingers ached. She shuddered as Technicolor images flashed through her mind like scenes from the late, late show: Jerry chasing her down the hall, Jerry dragging her back to the living room, cursing her, shaking her, hitting her. His eyes had been filled with violence, and his cruel words chosen to hurt. She flinched as she remembered the sound of his fist connecting with her cheekbone and felt the shattering pain.

"There's this wall along the front of my beach house. It's like these windows—floor-to-ceiling glass—to take advantage of the view. I remember heading toward it."

Despite the warmth of the fire, Savannah's blood had turned to ice. Her trembling increased, her eyes grew wide and dark. She could see Jerry's handsome face, now ugly and twisted with fury, she could smell the acrid odor of male sweat, taste her own blood, feel his fingers—as strong as steel—digging painfully into her shoulders. She could hear the sound of her scream.

"That's the last thing I remember until I woke up in the hospital the next morning."

"That's probably a good thing," Blake said. The memory of diving headfirst through a wall of glass would have to be horrific. Growing up on the rough side of life, Blake had never owned a pair of rose-colored glasses. He knew firsthand how ugly life could be. How violent. And how cruel. Very little shocked him. But the thought of Savannah, lying on the sand, alone and frail and broken, made him angry. More than angry. It made him furious.

She thought back to the panic she'd felt when she woke up in the hospital unable to feel her arms or her legs. There'd been only a dull, distant pain and the deep numbing sensation created by the painkillers and sedatives pumping through her bloodstream.

"I know he tried to kill me," she said in a small voice. Her throat was so tight that it hurt even to whisper. At first she'd thought she was going to die, and later, when the doctor cut back on the painkillers to keep her from becoming addicted, she'd wanted to die. But she hadn't. She'd survived, and although the doctors had finally proclaimed her cured, she still suffered nightmares and the occasional panic attacks.

Her eyes were burning with hot tears; Savannah resolutely blinked them away. It was too late for weeping. "But there was no proof of premeditation, so in the end, he plea-bargained to aggravated assault and was sentenced to a year in prison."

Blake did some quick mental calculation. "Which means he'll be getting out soon."

"Yes." She didn't say anything more. There was no need.

Swearing softly, he stood and crossed the room. When he took her in his arms, Savannah didn't resist. Instead, she rested her head against the solid strength of his shoulder.

They remained that way for a long, silent time. As he felt her trembling slowly begin to cease, Blake thought how good it felt to hold her like this, how perfectly her head nestled against his shoulder, how her soft, feminine body seemed to have melted into his.

Savannah was thinking that Blake was even more dangerous when he was being warm and caring. Part of her wished that she could spend the rest of her life in the protective circle of his strong arms. Another, more realistic part of her realized that to be totally dependent on any man, even this one, would be a fatal mistake. But for now, she couldn't think of any good reason to move.

Blake found himself wishing he'd thought to turn on some music. Something slow, deep and pulsing. He'd never been a man to worry about setting the scene for romance. Nor had any of his women ever seemed to need a scene set. That was something for the movies. At least it had been. Until now. Until this woman had come into his life and blurred the lines between fantasy and reality. Between desire and need.

Whatever game she was playing, whoever Savannah Starr was pretending to be, whatever lies she'd told to ensure that he'd give her his film to score—all that no longer mattered. He wanted her. And that enormous truth overrode everything else.

It was so quiet. There was only the soft sound of the rain on the roof, the crackling of the fire. And the beat of her heart. From the way it was pounding in her breast, Savannah was amazed Blake couldn't hear it in the stillness of the night.

"This is impossible," she murmured, even as she wrapped her arms more tightly around his waist.

Blake pressed his lips against her hair and inhaled the fresh scent of wildflowers. "Nothing's impossible."

"It can't go anywhere."

He shifted his attention to her earlobe. "It already has." He trailed his lips from her temple to her mouth. "I want you, Savannah." His breath was a warm breeze against her parted lips.

Her resolve was melting away, like a sand castle at high tide. She lifted her hands to his shoulders—whether to push him away or draw her closer, Savannah's turmoiled mind couldn't decide.

"No," she whispered.

As his stroking hand moved down her back, Savannah suddenly understood the appeal that had kept the Dracula myth alive through the centuries. The dark night-stalker was so very male. So very powerful. So dangerously erotic. And even as a woman knew she should ward him off, she couldn't help wondering what it would be like to have him make love to her.

"Blake—" Her planned words of protest stuck in her throat as he brushed his lips over her temple.

Blake heard the hesitancy in her voice, he saw the clouded confusion in her eyes. All the other women in his life had approached this moment with a casual aura of expectancy, of experience. None of them—until Savannah—had ever trembled in his arms.

Needs hammered at him. Along with a sudden panic that he wouldn't be—couldn't be—gentle enough. The emotional tug-of-war raging inside him was a new and unwelcome sensation. He lifted her hand to his mouth and kissed her fingers one by one. He looked directly into her eyes.

"I've been honest with you, Savannah. I've told you that I wanted you from the beginning."

It was seduction—his deep voice, the practiced touch of his hand, the hypnotic power of his midnight-dark eyes. What frightened Savannah was that even as she recognized it for what it was, she also found it inescapable. The last time she'd felt this helpless was when—

No! When he pressed his lips against her palm, she jerked away.

"Do you always get everything you want?"

She was rigid. Blake saw the fear in her eyes and understood it. He was suddenly feeling it himself. "Not always."

Emotions were tumbling around inside her. Confusion. Desire. Fear. Excitement. "I'm afraid."

"I know." He reached out and smoothed away the line between her brows. "I'd never hurt you, Savannah."

She read the honest emotion in his eyes and knew that Blake believed he was telling the truth. But he was wrong. Because if she allowed this to happen, she would be hurt. But dear Lord, even that inescapable knowledge didn't stop her from wanting him.

As he gathered her back into his arms, Savannah could have pulled away. She could have. Perhaps she even should have. But all she knew was that at that moment, making love with this man seemed almost predestined. And incredibly right. She fought to keep a rein on her emotions, but try as she might, her grip just kept slipping away.

"I don't know if I can give you what you want," she said quietly. "It's been so long, and I never was very experienced, and—"

"Shh." Lowering his head, Blake brushed his lips against hers, tempting, tantalizing, tormenting. It was more a promise than a proper kiss—a slow, alluring hint of pleasures to come. "Don't worry about me. All you have to do is take."

Slowly, thoroughly, with great skill and even greater patience, he seduced her solely with his mouth. His lips were firm, but surprisingly soft. And infinitely persuasive.

Savannah no longer had the strength to resist. Her body warmed, her mind emptied. Her head fell back and with a soft sigh, she bared her slender neck in erotic surrender.

6

KISSING SAVANNAH was like partaking of a feast after a long fast. Fighting for patience, Blake forced himself to go slowly. His mouth drank from hers with a gentleness he hadn't known he possessed; his hands moved up and down her back, his fingers dancing along the delicate bones of her spine in gestures meant to soothe even as they sought to arouse.

Kissing Blake was like falling into a dream. A blissfully sensual dream. Soft lights the color of precious gemstones—radiant ruby, shimmering sapphire, iridescent emerald—danced behind her closed lids.

Savannah wanted to think, to analyze every dazzling sensation, to ensure that later she'd remember everything about this moment. But as the tip of his tongue teased its way between her lips, she discovered that it was only possible to experience. To feel.

She felt the floor tilt beneath her. She swayed. Her fingers tightened on his shoulders, her body curved against his, her soft sigh was muffled by his mouth.

They drew apart in unspoken agreement. He cupped her chin, his fingers strong and possessive, but heartbreakingly tender. "I've never wanted a woman like I want you," he said.

His deep voice, the smoldering heat of his gaze, his warm touch against her skin, all conspired to thrill her.

Allowing herself to drown in the depths of Blake's eyes, Savannah surrendered to the inevitable.

When he went to lift her into his arms, Savannah murmured a soft protest. "No. Here," she answered his severe, questioning look. "Now. In front of the fire. Before I come to my senses."

Blake's relief was palpable. They knelt on the rug, thighs almost touching. His fingers explored the planes of her face. "You are exquisite."

As she felt his touch skim over her scar, Savannah turned her head away. This glorious, reckless moment was one she would remember all her life. She wanted it to be perfect. *She* wanted to be perfect. More than perfect. She wanted to be the most beautiful woman Blake had ever made love to.

Blake had never considered himself a particularly sensitive person, but he would have had to have been dense as a stone not to understand some of what Savannah was feeling.

"Don't turn away from me, Savannah."

She forced herself to meet what she knew would be his patiently sympathetic gaze. "I haven't been with a man for a long time. Not since . . ."

He ran his hand down her hair. "I won't hurt you."

"I know." Her eyes were glistening with tears she had never allowed herself to shed. "But there's something else. I have all these ugly scars," she managed on a strangled sob. "And I'm afraid when you see them, you won't want me anymore." Humiliated by the way she was ruining what had been a magical moment, she buried her face in her hands.

He parted the ebony curtain of hair veiling her face. "They don't matter. Not to me."

Gently, tenderly, Blake pried her fingers away from her face, one at a time, kissing each in turn. Then, taking hold of the bottom of her sweater, he pulled it over her head. Before she could protest, he was peeling her corduroy slacks down her bare legs.

She tried to turn away, but she was too late. He lowered his head and kissed her, effectively holding her hostage while his deft fingers unfastened the hooks at the back of her utilitarian white cotton bra.

In the amber glow of the firelight, she looked so fragile. And so beautiful. Although the light was dim, he could see a jagged line marching up the inside of her arm, a twin of those which twined around her thighs. There was another scar across her breast, dangerously close to her nipple.

"The plastic surgeons did a pretty good job on my face," she whispered. "But the others..." Her voice drifted off.

Desire warred with a murderous impulse—the need to comfort battled with the urge to drive to Sacramento, drag Larsen out of that cell where he was currently incarcerated and teach him the true meaning of pain. Moved too profoundly to speak, Blake lowered his head and kissed her wounded breast.

"There are scars, and there are scars, sweetheart," he said. "And believe me, yours aren't anything to write home about."

Savannah knew that he was talking about himself. She'd fallen through a window. But it seemed that

Blake, during his relationship with Pamela, had fallen into hell.

Her hands went to his shirt, struggling to undo the buttons as her gaze held his. But her fingers had turned to stone. Finally, frustrated, she gave up and yanked, causing buttons to scatter over the floor.

Finally! Heady with relief, Savannah pushed Blake's shirt off his shoulders. His dark skin gleamed in the firelight. Unable to resist, she reached out and touched him. His flesh beneath her stroking fingers was soft and smooth. But the muscle beneath was hard and wire-taut. Savannah pressed her lips against that warm, moist flesh, drinking in its texture, its taste, his earthy male scent.

She was amazing, Blake thought dizzily. Hadn't it been just moments ago that he'd been worried about comforting her? About assuring her that he found her unflawed?

So how had the tables so devastatingly turned? How was it that with just the delicate touch of her hands, the feel of her lips against his skin, she was driving him beyond reason?

Outside the rain continued. Inside, a raging storm swirled. There was thunder. Savannah felt it when her lips skimmed over Blake's heart. There was lightning. She saw it in his eyes. Overcome with a heady sense of feminine power, Savannah laughed.

The throaty sound tolled in his head. At thirty-three, none of Blake's eighteen years of sexual experience could have remotely prepared him for this. For Savannah.

When her tongue trailed wetly down his chest, something in Blake snapped. Patience was forgotten. He pulled her against him, his hands greedy, his mouth hungry. In turn, Savannah arched against him, offering, challenging, daring.

The last of their clothes were whipped away, as if by gale-force winds. The storm—already all-consuming— intensified. If Blake was crazed, Savannah was obsessed.

He was a ruthless lover—wild, demanding, driving her toward delirium as he turned her in his arms, bending her to his will, tasting every fragrant bit of exposed flesh. But Savannah, feeling alive for the first time in more than a year, didn't want gentleness.

She clung to him, her nails digging into him, her legs wrapped like a vise around his hips, her mind cleared of anything but swirling sensations and a blinding pleasure just this side of pain.

His clever hands and wicked lips were never still as he drove her higher and higher, closer and closer to oblivion. And then she was tumbling over the edge, shuddering as climax after extraordinary climax slammed through her.

Blake watched her dazed eyes fly open. He heard her gasp his name. He held her until the wild tremors passed.

"You are incredible," he murmured against her mouth. "Absolutely incredible."

Savannah lay limp in his arms. She'd never known it was possible to feel so much. And then, to her amazement, it was happening again. All it took was the lightest of touches to make her arousal burst free again. As

Blake slid his moist body over her love-slick flesh, Savannah was stunned by the way he could send passion throbbing through her so soon again. She took him into her. Deeply. Fully.

His hands linked with hers. Their fingers tightened. Rhythms matched. Outside the windows a full white moon rose. And so did they.

IT WAS THE SILENCE that woke her. The steady sound of the rain, which had infiltrated its way into her sleep, had stopped. Savannah lay alone in the bed, momentarily disoriented by her strange surroundings. Then she remembered.

She was in Blake's bed. She recalled him carrying her down the curving staircase after they'd made love in front of the fire. That had only been the first time. Displaying a stamina that was nearly superhuman, Blake had taught Savannah exactly how responsive her body could be as he'd stroked and coaxed her to euphoric heights of ecstasy.

In return, he'd held nothing back, encouraging Savannah's exploring hands and lips to grow more and more intrepid until she'd learned to read his needs and desires as a blind woman would read Braille.

Every intimate aspect of the love-filled night flooded her mind, sensual flashbacks vying with embarrassment at her total loss of restraint. She closed her eyes, rubbing her fingers across her lids until she could see stars dancing against a background of black velvet.

What had she done? Spent the night with a man she'd only known twenty-four short hours. At the time, everything had seemed brushed with a romantic golden glow; but now, in the cold light of day, Savannah wished that she'd stuck to her guns and refused to consider Justin's proposition.

But then she would have missed a unique opportunity: the chance to score Blake's brilliant film—a film that could easily earn them both another Oscar.

The thing to do, Savannah decided as she pushed aside the tangled sheets and climbed out of the antique sleigh bed on legs that felt unusually stiff and sore, was to put last night behind her and move on.

She'd simply explain to Blake that although he was a marvelous lover, she wasn't in the market for any entanglements right now. It was important, for the sake of the work, that they keep their relationship strictly business.

She continued to give herself that little pep talk as she showered and dressed. Following the enticing scent of coffee, she headed toward the kitchen, relieved when she only got lost once along the way.

A brief note beside the enormous brass espresso maker/coffee brewer told her that Blake was down on the beach. The note didn't invite her to join him.

Deciding not to wait for an invitation, Savannah retrieved the slicker from the brass coatrack in the foyer and headed down the narrow tree-lined path to the sea.

The coast wore its morning gray coat of fog. It moved across the damp sand like low-lying clouds, making ordinary things—rocks, driftwood and stunted, twisted trees—into objects of mystery.

"Keep going in that direction and you're going to run into a dead end." The fog's odd acoustic quality made the deep male voice sound as if it were coming from right behind her.

Savannah turned around, watching Blake emerge from the filmy gray shadows, as silent as a cat on a plush carpet. "The tide's coming in," he explained. "It's easy to get stranded."

She pushed her hands deep into her pockets. "Thanks for the warning."

Blake hated the way something inside him had moved as he'd stood in the narrow cove and watched Savannah making her way over the rock-strewn sands. He'd hoped that once he'd made love to her, once he'd satiated the desire he'd been unwillingly harboring for weeks, he'd have her out of his system, out of his mind. That had been his plan. But like so many best-laid plans, it hadn't worked out that way.

Instead, as his gaze roamed her face, taking in the soft shadows beneath her eyes—mute proof of the way they'd spent the night—and her bruised lips, whose taste he could still taste, even now, Blake found himself wanting her more than ever.

"You're up early," he said. His mouth was unsmiling, set in a grim line that was every bit as cold as the morning sea air.

"So are you."

Although they were only a few feet apart, an emotional chasm as deep and as wide as the Grand Canyon had opened up between them. Savannah searched his eyes for answers and found none. Was he angry? Was he regretting what had happened last night? Did he still believe that she was the type of woman who'd sleep with him in order to score his film?

Blake shrugged. "I'm not much for sleeping in."

His eyes were unfathomable black wells; his remote tone, worlds different from the lush voice that had caressed her senses long into the early hours of the morning. Savannah told herself that she should be grateful that he'd gone back to his impersonal, distant self. It would make her insistence on a business-only relationship that much easier.

"Neither am I."

They didn't speak for a long, nerve-racking time. Out over the icy waters, gulls dove for fish, their querulous cries echoing in the fog.

Blake had slept fitfully, awakening before dawn. Loath to leave the warm bed, and Savannah, he'd known that to stay would represent emotional perils he wasn't prepared to face. So he'd sat in a chair beside the bed, watching Savannah sleep. And as the frail yellow light of the rising sun gradually filtered into his bedroom, he'd seen the bruises on her arms, her shoulders. And although the thought made him sick at heart, he knew that if he'd pulled the rumpled sheets away, he would have seen identical bruises darkening the soft skin of her thighs.

He'd left the room to walk along the kelp-strewn beach, lambasting himself for his lack of finesse. He'd wanted her, and he wasn't about to apologize for that. But the bruises—they were another story altogether. He'd never hurt a woman. Not even Pamela, although there had admittedly been times, when she'd been taunting him relentlessly, that he'd been tempted.

"About last night." He continued to look out over the steely, white-capped waves. "I'm sorry."

He could have said nothing worse. "You don't owe me an apology, Blake."

Damn. Blake watched the pain flood into her eyes and wondered what he'd done wrong now. "Whatever you think of me, I didn't mean to hurt you, Savannah."

Savannah didn't answer. Instead, she jammed her hands even deeper into her slicker pockets and tried to remain calm.

"You were upset after telling me about Larsen," Blake said. "I took advantage of that. I also was rougher than I should have been. Than I wanted to be. And for that I'm sorry."

Savannah conveniently forgot that she hadn't felt exactly jubilant about what had happened between them herself. Instead, her injured pride caused her to retreat into herself. Unable to meet his gaze, she looked out over the sea.

The waves were crashing against the rugged granite cliff. Dark green seaweed swirled in the frothy surf and was scattered over the rocky shoreline. Savannah had always loved living at the beach; she'd loved the tranquillity of the never-ending tide, the golden expanse of gleaming, sunlit sand. But this was different. There was nothing tranquil about Blake's ocean. It stormed angrily against the rocks, presenting challenge. And danger.

"I wasn't so upset about Jerry that I didn't know what I was doing," she said finally. Was that calm voice really hers?

"I still can't remember when I've taken a woman with less care," Blake said grimly. "My God, Savannah, I practically ripped your clothes off."

"Actually, if I remember correctly, I ripped your shirt off," Savannah reminded him. "It was your apology that hurt me, Blake. After all, we're both adults, and last night's lovemaking—sex—" she corrected briskly "—was mutual. It was also no big deal." She held her breath, waiting irrationally for a bolt of lightning to come out of the leaden sky and strike her down for telling such an outrageous lie.

Blake hadn't known what to expect. Anger? Tears? Recriminations? He'd been prepared to handle any of those. But never in a million years had he expected Savannah's cool rejection of what they'd shared. Forgetting that ten minutes ago all he'd wanted was to get off the hook, he now found her uncaring attitude more than a little irritating.

"That's funny," he ground out. "I had the impression that what we shared last night was more than just a casual roll in the hay." The stiff sea breeze blew several errant strands of dark hair against her cheek; his fingers practically itched with the need to reach out and touch her, to brush it away.

His scorn stung. And although his tone was as sharp as a slap, Savannah refused to flinch. Tossing her hair out of her face, she glared up at him. "It was. Whatever else you think of me, Blake, I've never gone in for casual sex. I was merely trying to explain that I understand how you feel. It's been a long time for both of us and last night, partly because of your film and partly because of the rain, we were both feeling a little down.

It was probably inevitable that we'd end up in bed together."

Personally, Blake had awakened with the uneasy feeling that it was a great deal more complicated than Savannah was making it out to be. But since he wasn't at all eager to muddy already-dangerous waters, he decided not to argue. "I suppose that makes sense."

"Of course it does."

Savannah wondered whether Blake was really that dense or merely the most adept liar she'd ever met. Because although neither one of them wanted to admit it, they both knew that something serious had happened last night. Something irrevocable. Something she'd have to think about. As soon as she returned home to Malibu.

"Believe me, Blake," she continued earnestly, "I am not so desperate for a man—even a man who's a dynamite lover—that I'd wake up expecting a proposal."

He should have felt relief. Instead, he felt inexplicably frustrated. Shaking off the errant thought, he asked, "Am I, really?"

"What?"

"A dynamite lover."

It was the one thing Savannah knew she'd never get away with lying about. Because her body had told him the truth in more ways than one. Her reminiscent smile was genuine. "The best."

That, at least, was something, Blake decided. Her next statement jolted him back to reality.

"And now that we understand one another, I think it's time for me to go back to Malibu."

"Are you saying you've changed your mind about scoring my film?"

"Of course not."

"You don't trust me." *Worse*, Blake considered grimly. After the rough way he'd treated her, she was probably afraid of him. And no wonder, considering her brutal experience with Larsen.

"It doesn't have anything to do with trust," she insisted, not quite truthfully. Savannah didn't think it prudent to add that she couldn't trust herself to stay under the same roof with Blake without becoming emotionally and physically involved. "It's just that I can work better in my own home."

No. Dammit, she wasn't going anywhere. She was staying here. With him, where she belonged. Realizing that if he said his thoughts out loud, he'd sound exactly like the murderously possessive Jerry Larsen, Blake bit back a furious retort and forced a shrug.

"Whatever you want. Since my film is in dire need of a score, I wouldn't think of depriving you of your muse."

As they walked back up the beach together, Savannah knew that she should be glad about his easy acceptance. For a moment, she'd thought she'd seen a flash of all-too-familiar anger in his dark eyes. But obviously, she'd been wrong. Because Blake didn't seem to care where she worked. So long as she came through with a score that would enhance his movie.

She should be relieved, Savannah told herself. So why did she feel so depressed?

ALTHOUGH SHE HAD LEFT Blake miles away in Mendocino, Savannah couldn't expunge him from her mind. She thought about him constantly, from the moment she woke up until she went to bed. And even as she tried to tell herself that such thoughts were only normal— after all, she was spending ten to twelve hours a day working on the score of his incredibly personal film— she couldn't quite make herself believe that her interest in the man was purely professional.

Her emotions were in turmoil, but instead of shutting them off, she used them, focusing her tumultuous feelings on her work. Passion, anger, fear, pride, torment. The vibrant physical feelings flowed hotly in her blood, escaping through her fingertips, racing over the synthesizer keyboard, pouring into her music as she composed a swelling score to fit with Blake's equally intense scenes.

The first morning after her return to Malibu, a florist's delivery woman arrived on Savannah's doorstep with a single white rose. Although there was no card, Savannah knew that the rose was from Blake. Perhaps he was thinking about her, too. The idea of him pacing the beach, unable to get her out of his mind, was undeniably appealing.

A second rose arrived that afternoon. A third in the evening. Even as she responded to Blake's renewed seduction attempts, she couldn't quite forget the look on his face when he apologized so brusquely for making love to her. Besides, if he'd really wanted her to stay, he would have asked. Wouldn't he?

IT WAS NIGHT. Savannah was standing in the center of the room, her nude body glistening in the pale silver moonlight. A man approached. Beneath a raven-black widow's peak his dark eyes blazed with hunger. Some last vestige of self-protection told Savannah that she should run away—now, while she had the chance. But she remained rooted to the spot, entranced by the pull of those fathomless eyes.

He didn't speak. Instead, he simply held out his arms in invitation. Her knees trembling with each step, Savannah walked toward him, unable to resist his silent appeal. He wrapped his arms around her, enfolding her in his voluminous black cape. As she tilted her head back, exposing the long white column of her throat, Savannah was trembling with passion and anticipation.

Just as his teeth grazed her proffered flesh, the telephone rang. And rang. And rang. Fighting to struggle free from the erotic dream, Savannah groped blindly for the receiver.

"Hello?"

No one answered.

"Hello?"

When the voice on the other end remained stubbornly mute, Savannah was forced to wonder if she was still dreaming. She dragged her free hand across her face, struggling to wake up.

"Who is this?" she demanded, imagining that she could hear the caller breathing. "Blake? Is that you?"

She couldn't help wondering if he was checking to see if she was at home. The same way Jerry Larsen had done during those months they'd been dating. The very idea made her slam the receiver back down onto its cradle.

Although she'd left her dream at a particularly frustrating stage, further sleep proved impossible. Savannah went around the house, checking locks and turning on all the lights. Then she sat alone in the predawn darkness, her arms wrapped around herself, willing the sun to rise.

THE ROSES CONTINUED for another two days. As did the middle-of-the-night phone calls. Having vowed never to be a victim again, Savannah called Blake's home to insist that he stop harassing her.

"I'm sorry, ma'am," the male operator informed her, "but that line has been out of order for the past three days."

"Are you certain the phone hasn't been working at least part of the time?" she asked hopefully. As frightening as the idea of Blake making those calls was, the idea that it might *not* be him was even more terrifying.

There was a brief silence during which time Savannah could hear the unmistakable tapping of a computer keyboard. "No," he assured her. "The line's completely dead. We've been having a lot of storms," he added.

"Oh. Well, thanks for your help."

"No problem, ma'am. Have a nice day."

Frustrated, Savannah hung up and tried to return to work. But creativity was impossible. Because all she could think about was some unseen person outside her home, silently stalking her, waiting for just the right moment to make his move.

BLAKE WAS GOING CRAZY. In a way, he was almost grateful that the phone was out of order. Because he wouldn't know what to say to Savannah if he did get hold of her. The first day after her departure, he'd fully expected her to return. By the second day, he'd decided that fate had stepped in and downed the telephone lines to keep him from making a fool of himself. After all, he assured himself, sooner or later, she'd be back.

By the third day, he'd come to the conclusion that if Savannah did show up, he'd be tempted to wring her gorgeous neck for driving him insane this way.

After three days of cursing Savannah, cursing himself, Blake paced along the widow's walk, glaring out over the sea. From this vantage point he could see the fishing boats steaming along the horizon, trailing their nets behind them, and the buoys bobbing on the swelling waves, marking their path. He watched the gulls as they dove into the water, emerging seconds later with flashes of silver in their beaks. He could see for miles. But not far enough—because he couldn't see Savannah.

Even as he blamed Savannah for his insane behavior, Blake couldn't help wondering if this strange, unsettling feeling he was experiencing was loneliness. It couldn't be. After all, he'd lived alone for years. He'd been alone—both emotionally and physically—most of his life. And since the one time he had made the mistake of allowing a woman to infringe on his solitude, he'd gotten burned, Blake reminded himself that he'd vowed, Never again. He preferred a life without strings. Without commitment.

So, why the hell was he feeling so rotten? As much as he hated to admit it, Blake knew that the reason that he was acting like a maniac was because he missed Savannah.

"Double, double toil and trouble," Cujo croaked.

"You can say that again, pal," Blake muttered.

Giving up, as he'd known all along he would, Blake went inside to his bedroom and tossed a few essentials into a duffel bag.

As he drove down the winding coast highway toward the San Francisco airport, Blake considered blackly that there was a very thin line between want and need. And although it was an unwelcome thought, he wondered if he'd already crossed it.

7

ALTHOUGH SHE HAD NEVER considered herself the least bit psychic, the moment the bell chimed, Savannah knew precisely who was on the other side of her door. One look through the peephole confirmed her intuition. She took her time unfastening the locks.

"You have one hell of a nerve," she flared after she flung open the door.

Blake took one look at her and realized he hadn't imagined her beauty, after all. He'd promised himself that he wouldn't let himself fall for her feminine charms, yet he was being drawn in deeper every time he saw her.

"Anyone ever tell you that you are gorgeous when angry?"

"I'd think a brilliant screenwriter such as yourself could come up with a better opening line than that one."

"I probably could," he agreed easily. "But it wouldn't be as accurate." Without waiting for an invitation, he moved past her into her house. "What's got you so hot under the collar, anyway?"

Frustrated, she slammed the door behind him. Blake watched without comment as she refastened each heavy lock, one by one. When the task was completed, she turned on him, her hands curled into fists at her hips, her eyes shooting furious sparks. Blake had a sudden urge to kiss her.

"As if you didn't know." She practically spat the words at him. "I was ready to take out a restraining order on you."

"On me? Why?"

As an actress, Savannah knew that there were two emotions difficult to fake: grief and astonishment. And at this moment, the latter was etched into every line of Blake's face.

"Because of the roses," she said with a bit less assurance. "Although I have to admit that I found them rather appealing in the beginning, after a while the novelty pales. As for the phone calls—"

"Wait a minute." Blake held up a hand. "What roses are you talking about?"

"You know very well what roses. The white ones. The ones you sent."

Damn. He should have sent flowers, Blake realized. After the night they'd shared, it would have been the gentlemanly thing to do. But, unaccustomed to courting a woman, he hadn't.

"I didn't send you any roses, Savannah."

She folded her arms across her chest. "I suppose you're also going to deny making those phone calls."

"I thought about calling you. But I couldn't. The lines were out. Because of the storm," he tacked on, confirming what the operator had already told her.

The bright scarlet in Savannah's cheeks drained away. "If you're not telling the truth, so help me, I'll..."

She dragged an unsteady hand through her hair. "I don't know what I'll do," she managed in a fractured voice. "But I promise you, Blake, it won't be pretty."

She wasn't angry any longer. Instead, she seemed to be frightened. Correction, Blake thought as he took her trembling hand between both of his and found it to be ice cold. She was terrified.

"I wouldn't lie to you, Savannah. Not about this."

Her eyes searched his face, looking for answers. "If it wasn't you . . ." Her voice drifted off. The alternative was too horrible to consider.

"I think I'd better call the police," she said, after she'd told Blake what had been happening ever since she'd returned home.

He nodded, unnerved to discover that his own blood was running disturbingly cold. "I think that's a very good idea. Where's your kitchen?"

She was surprised by the sudden change in subject. "It's through those swinging doors. Why?"

"I thought I'd make you some tea. Unless you'd prefer something stronger."

"Nothing alcoholic, thank you." Savannah wanted her wits about her when she talked with Mike McAllister, the detective who had handled her case last year. "But tea sounds great."

When Blake returned to the living room, fragile china teacup in hand, he found Savannah standing by the glass wall, staring out over the vast expanse of Pacific Ocean. The Southern California sunlight had tinted the foaming whitecaps a brilliant gold that was vastly different from the steely, storm-tossed waves Blake was used to viewing from his windows. It was almost impossible to believe they were part of the same ocean.

It was also difficult to believe that evil things such as brutal murder attempts could happen in such a bright, sunlit paradise. But they did. Savannah had the scars to prove it.

"That was a short phone call," he said.

Her face, as she turned toward him, was as white as a wraith's. "Mike McAllister, the detective who originally handled my case, is on vacation. Which I suppose explains why I wasn't notified immediately." She took a deep, shuddering breath. "He was released last week. While I was in Mendocino with you."

Blake didn't need to ask who she was talking about. "Larsen."

Savannah tried to push the answer past the lump in her throat and failed. Instead, all she could do was nod.

"That settles it," he said. "You're coming back to Mendocino with me."

As much as Savannah wanted to run away from Jerry Larsen, to hide somewhere safe where he could never find her, never hurt her, some faint voice in the far reaches of her mind reminded her that a danger of another kind waited for her at Blake's home.

"I can't."

She was strong. That she'd survived such terror was proof of both her strength and her ability to take care of herself. But her soft brown eyes looked so haunted that Blake knew he'd do whatever it took to protect her from further pain.

"Of course, you can. I have everything you need to work. And you'll be safe. I'll protect you."

"I see. And what will you be doing while I'm scoring your picture?" Savannah asked. "Hunting woolly mammoths for our dinner?"

If the subject under discussion hadn't been so serious, Blake would have enjoyed her pointed accusation. All right, so he was old-fashioned enough to believe that a man's job was to protect the weaker sex whenever necessary. Was that honestly so terrible?

"First a vampire, then a Neanderthal. You really know how to flatter a guy, Savannah."

"If the animal skin fits—" The chime of the doorbell interrupted her.

"I'll get it," Blake said, moving toward the front door before Savannah had a chance to protest.

He was back in a minute with yet another white rose. Savannah noticed that the crystal vase looked particularly delicate in his dark hand. His scowl was as threatening as any she had witnessed.

"How long will it take you to pack?"

"I'm not going anywhere."

"The hell, you're not." He shoved the flower toward her. "Look at it carefully, Savannah. And then tell me that you want to hang around here, waiting for the guy to show."

At first glance the rose looked exactly like the other. "Pull back the petals," Blake instructed.

She did, gasping when she saw the pearly head of a long slender pin inserted into the snowy bud.

"Just because the guy didn't kill you the first time, is no reason to give him a second chance."

Savannah stood up very straight. "I hadn't realized that writing a television cop show made you an expert on the criminal mind."

Blake was momentarily thrown off track by her reference to his work. "Not many people remember that show."

"I loved *Police Beat*. In fact, I never missed it. Even when it cost me an A in calculus." At his puzzled look, Savannah elaborated. "Remember that two-parter you did, about the wife who hid her daughter from her former husband because she couldn't get anyone to believe that he'd been sexually abusing the little girl during visitations?"

"I remember." Blake also remembered the blazing arguments he'd had with the network censors in order to get that particular show on the air.

"The second episode ran the night I was supposed to be cramming for a midterm my freshman year at USC," Savannah explained. "But since I had to know how the story ended, I decided to blow off the exam. I ended up getting my only C." She smiled. "But it was definitely worth it."

Blake wanted to return her smile. But he couldn't. Because of the damn rose. "If you never missed a show, you'll undoubtedly recall the episode where the guy killed his wife after she asked for a divorce."

"I remember it."

"Then you should also understand why we have to get you away from town," Blake said in a no-nonsense voice Savannah was beginning to recognize.

"I can't hide away in Mendocino forever."

"You don't have to. Only until the police can find Larsen and discover whether or not he's your secret admirer and tongue-shy midnight caller."

Although she hated to admit it, he had a point. "I have to warn you, I don't know how to handle being protected."

"Don't worry. You'll get used to it."

The was exactly what Savannah was afraid of. It hadn't been easy, living alone after what had happened to her. If she were to be perfectly honest, she'd still admit that sometimes, late at night, the sound of the wind against the windows or a car pulling into her driveway to turn around made her want to call 911. But she was becoming stronger—braver—with each passing day. And she was damned if she was going to allow Jerry Larsen to turn her into a cowering, terrified victim.

What Blake said made a great deal of sense, though. "All right," she said reluctantly. "But this time, things are going to be strictly business."

As he thought about Larsen lurking somewhere out there, prepared to hurt Savannah again, Blake knew that he'd do whatever it took to keep her safe. He considered assuring her that he had no intention of making love to her again, but knew that would be a lie.

"I promise not to do anything you don't want," he said instead.

"That's not good enough." Because the mere proximity of this man was enough to erode her distressingly crumbling willpower.

Conflict raged in him. He wanted her. He wanted to get away from her. What he was, dammit, Blake realized, was trapped.

"What do you want me to do? Lie and tell you that I don't want you? That I haven't spent the last three nights thinking of you, remembering your taste, your scent, how good you felt in my arms? The way everything between us was such a close and perfect fit?"

Bridging the gap between them, he took a strand of her hair and wrapped it around his hand. "When you were staying at my house, I could think of nothing but you. Oh, I assured myself that once you returned to Malibu, I'd come to my senses and realize that I'd only exaggerated my feelings. But I was wrong. Because after you left, I found myself thinking of you when I should have been thinking of other things.

"Dammit, I want you, Savannah. I want you in my bed. I want to make love to you all night long. In front of the fire, until all the logs have burned down to embers. Until your body and your mind are filled with me."

Ignoring her quick, involuntary gasp, he tugged on her hair, drawing her even closer. "Only me."

Her stomach was knotted with tension, her heartbeat accelerated, but a strange excitement swam in her head. "What about what *I* want?" Savannah tossed back. "Don't my feelings count for anything?"

Blake couldn't recall the last time he'd been this frustrated. "Of course they do."

"Then you'll understand when I tell you that the only relationship I want to share with you is a professional one." That was a lie. She cared. And because she cared, she was too vulnerable for her own good.

"Fine. So, since you appear to be a very strong-willed lady and I'm not the kind of man to force a woman into my bed, there's no reason why you shouldn't come back to my place."

He had, Savannah realized, backed her into a very tidy little corner. Worse yet, hearing her own logic thrown back in her face forced her to admit that she'd done it to herself.

"Don't tell me you're afraid," Blake challenged with a knowing smile.

"Of you? Of course not." Another lie. Because there was something dangerously exciting about the way this man could take her over, make her ache with need— something that was every bit as frightening as it was compelling.

"Good." He struggled to keep his face expression- less. "So, why don't you pack your clothes while I call the police department and tell them where you're go- ing to be. Who should I talk to?"

Annoyed by the way he was issuing orders like a drill sergeant, Savannah also wasn't all that eager to talk again with the detective who was handling Mike McAllister's cases. The man's tone, while polite enough, had been decidedly officious. As if *Dragnet*'s Sergeant Joe Friday had been his role model. From the way this latest rose had affected her nerves, she was afraid she'd come off sounding like a hysterical female victim. Something she never intended to be again.

"Lieutenant Peterson. The number's on a card by the phone. Oh, and Blake?"

He'd just begun to dial.

When he glanced up at her, Savannah said, "That scenario of yours, the one where we're making love in front of the fireplace?"

Just the thought was enough to cause his fingers to tighten on the receiver. "What about it?"

"I wouldn't hold your breath. Because it isn't going to happen."

"Of course it is." Unexpectedly, he flashed her a smile. "But I'm willing to wait until you admit that you want it, too."

His smile was quick and utterly charming. Savannah hated him for it. Anger, hot and fast, flared in her eyes. It flooded her cheeks.

"You're going to have a very long wait." She turned on her heel and marched out of the room.

Blake was a great deal more comfortable with Savannah's anger than he would have been with her surrender. Having struggled to the top the hard way, he'd learned to be suspicious of anything that came too easily.

"Oh, I am going to have you, Savannah," he murmured as he resumed punching the Lucite buttons. "And it isn't going to be nearly as long a wait as you think."

HER FIRST TWO DAYS in Mendocino proved to Savannah that it was a mistake to try and second-guess Blake Winters. All during the flight and then the long drive up the coast, she'd been afraid that the moment they were alone in his isolated house, he'd pounce.

But instead of attempting to initiate a sexual relationship, he kept an emotional distance from her that was proving as vast and remote as the Sahara Desert. And while she told herself that she should be grateful for his apparent lack of sexual interest, working closely together on such an intimate project without exchanging so much as a single casual word began to get on Savannah's nerves.

Adding to the tension was the unpalatable fact that Jerry Larsen had apparently disappeared from the face of the earth. After telling her that he'd missed his weekly appointment with his parole officer, the Los Angeles police had assured her that they were doing everything they could to locate him. Remembering how inefficient they'd been the last time Jerry had harassed her, Savannah was not encouraged.

On the morning of the second day after she'd returned to Blake's house, the phone rang. Since Blake was out walking on the beach, Savannah answered it.

"Hello?"

There was nothing but dead air on the other end of the line.

Savannah's fingers tightened around the receiver. "Hello?" It could have been her imagination, but she thought she heard breathing. "Who is this?"

Instead of an answer, the line went dead. Frozen to the spot, Savannah was still holding the receiver in her hand, staring at it, when Blake returned.

"What's wrong?" She was as pale as a wraith.

"Nothing." She was definitely overreacting, Savannah told herself. By letting her nerves get the best of her like this she was behaving like some airhead heroine in a teenage slasher movie. "It was only a wrong number."

"You were afraid it was him. Larsen."

His voice was calm and unemotional, exactly the way she needed it to be. "No." Savannah shook her head. "No," she repeated more firmly.

"We can call the local cops, if it'll make you feel better."

"Over a wrong number? You know as well as I do that they'd write the whole thing off to me being a hysterical female."

"They might take it more seriously than you think." Blake hadn't been able to get the mental picture of Savannah flying through the shattered glass out of his mind.

"I'm not running to the police every time something unexplainable happens," Savannah insisted in a voice that wasn't as strong as it might have been. "Jerry's already caused me enough harm. I refuse to give him the power to frighten me."

When Blake looked inclined to argue, Savannah went back to work, refusing to allow herself to dwell on Jerry Larsen's whereabouts.

She was good, Blake decided. Very good. But as skilled an actress as Savannah Starr was, he knew that whoever had been on the other end of the phone had given her one hell of a scare.

He wanted to touch her, to soothe her ragged nerves. But sensing that it was important for her to appear strong, he said nothing, even as he planned to call the L.A. police and tell them about the phone call. Just in case.

"I'm almost tempted to go back into acting," she said to Blake late in the afternoon of their fourth day together.

Blake glanced up from the Moviola where he was tinkering with what was supposed to be the final cut of *Unholy Matrimony*. As his gaze slid over her profile, Blake experienced the familiar low, sexual pull that was growing more painful with each passing day. He ignored it. For now.

"Don't tell me that you're missing the adulation already, Ms. Starr?"

She spun around and glared at him. "Not at all," she said between clenched teeth, strangely grateful for his sarcasm.

It was a great deal easier to remember that she had absolutely no intention of getting personally involved with the man when he was being so cynical.

"It's simply that good parts for actresses are few and far between, and this is the juiciest part since Kathleen Turner's role in *Body Heat*."

"I don't know," he drawled, rubbing his chin and looking at her thoughtfully. "I thought you did an admirable job with your last role."

"Ah, yes. The black widow."

Relaxing for a moment, Savannah leaned back in her chair and ran her hands idly through her hair. She was wearing it loose today; it had taken every ounce of Blake's restraint not to bury his hands into the fragrant ebony waves that tumbled over her shoulders.

"But as much fun as that woman was to play," Savannah said, "she was still pretty one-dimensional. I mean, let's face it, how many men would really commit murder for sex?"

At this moment, Blake could think of one. He hadn't had an easy moment since Savannah had first shown up, dripping wet, on his doorstep. The past few days, working in such close proximity with her, knowing that she was asleep just a few doors away at night, had played holy hell with his libido.

Once again, the image of Savannah as a siren came to mind. Savannah of the wide brown eyes and wet, tangled, gypsy hair; a smiling Savannah singing sweetly while she lured some hapless sailor toward a rocky coast. With a mighty effort, Blake steeled himself against her feminine charms, reminding himself of the dangers of being pulled in too deeply.

Not having expected an answer to what was a rhetorical question, Savannah continued her appraisal. "But your character is so wonderfully, frightfully fascinating. She's like a Venus flytrap. Beautiful, seductive, and deadly. Even when the hero realizes that she will be his downfall, he can't resist her fatal charms."

"Perhaps," Blake suggested, thinking back on the man he'd been when he'd first met Pamela, "he was too egotistical to see the danger."

Savannah considered that for a long, thoughtful minute. "Are you saying that he only saw what he wanted to see?"

"Doesn't everyone?"

They were no longer talking about the film. "Perhaps." The movement of her shoulders was noncommittal, but as her eyes met his, Savannah wondered what Blake saw when he looked at her.

When his gaze drifted to her mouth, the sudden revelation of desire she saw in those darkening eyes— after four days of agonizingly polite conversation— struck like a jagged bolt of lightning from a clear blue summer sky. Savannah lifted a hand to her throat in a flustered gesture.

"I'd better get to work." Willpower alone kept her voice steady.

Cujo, who'd taken to perching atop the television while Savannah worked, ruffled his dark wings. "Get thee to a nunnery."

Too late, Cujo, Savannah considered silently.

To her vast relief, Blake didn't comment on the bird's suggestive piece of advice. "You worked through lunch."

He'd put a sandwich and cinnamon-spiced tea on the table beside her but, lost in a private world of her own making, she'd ignored them. Finally, when the bread had hardened and the tea had turned cold, he'd taken them away. Savannah hadn't noticed.

"I'd say it's time you had a break." He stood. "Let's take a walk along the beach."

Her first impression of Blake Winters had been right on the mark. Oh, he might not be the black-caped Dracula of Hollywood horror movies, but in his own inimitable way, he was a very dangerous man.

He had a way of making her want things she'd convinced herself that she didn't want from a man. And he'd made her feel things she'd vowed never to feel again. Eager to escape the sudden intimacy drawing them together, Savannah quickly agreed.

The day had dawned cold and gray, and the pale late-afternoon sunshine filtering through the slate clouds added scant warmth. Whitecaps stormed against the rocks, their turbulence echoing the way Savannah had felt ever since meeting Blake.

"Cold?" When he saw her shiver, his hand closed over hers before she could object.

"Yes." Savannah looked up at him. "But I like it. It's stimulating."

"Talk about stimulating..." Blake ran his knuckles along the roses the brisk sea wind had caused to bloom in her cheek.

His soft touch warmed her to the core. Her heart pounded in her throat. She saw it coming and did nothing to stop it. Later, Savannah would curse herself for such uncharacteristic passivity. But, for the moment, all she could think of was how much she wanted Blake to kiss her.

Blake felt her breath tremble out, he heard her soft sigh against his mouth. The impulse that had led him to kiss her flared dangerously as her lips yielded to his. He'd expected her to resist. Then, after that initial resistance, he'd hoped for a display of the passion she'd revealed that stormy night they'd made love. But instead, she was so soft, so sweet, so tender, that he was struck with an overwhelming need to protect her.

The more she gave, the more Blake wanted. He ached for her—body, mind and soul. He wanted to drag her to the damp, tide-packed sand underfoot; her vulnerability prevented him. His blood swimming, he managed to put his hands on her shoulders and ease her away.

Feeling as if the sand had shifted beneath her feet, Savannah clung to him. "We shouldn't have done that."

Her ragged voice was nearly inaudible over the roar of the surf and the pounding of his heart. "Give me one reason why not."

A thousand reasons tumbled wildly through her mind. Savannah latched on to the most obvious. "It isn't safe."

"So, who needs safe?"

When he went to touch her cheek again, she took a step backward. Physically and emotionally. "I do."

Blake couldn't remember when he'd met a woman who intrigued him more. Savannah was strong; the way she'd survived the horror Jerry Larsen had inflicted and gone on to pick up the threads of her life again was proof of that. But she was also fragile. The combination of strength and vulnerability would have been appealing enough. But mix into it the passion lurking beneath her controlled surface and Savannah Starr was irresistible.

So many layers, he mused. It could take a man a very long time to peel them each off, one by one. Even as he knew the dangers of becoming too involved, Blake found himself looking forward to the challenge.

"Yes." He spoke quietly, more to himself than to her. "You would." His gaze was steady, telling her that he was prepared to wait.

He wanted to kiss her again. Badly. But he forced himself to resist the temptation. Instead, he simply reached down, took her hand and laced their fingers together.

Relieved that Blake seemed willing to back away from what had been a very tempting situation, Savannah made the mistake of relaxing as they walked back up the beach, hand in hand.

They had almost reached the house when Blake said, "Soon you're going to realize that you'll always be safe with me, Savannah."

It had been too long since he'd kissed her—almost five minutes. Blake bent his head and brushed his lips against hers. The kiss was feather soft and unthreatening. But no less satisfying. "And when you do, we're going to make love."

For some reason, this time his aura of masculine confidence didn't irritate her. Instead, she smiled. "You don't give up easily, do you?"

The look he gave her was as serious as any she'd seen. "When it's something—or someone—I want? Never."

As they entered the house, Savannah couldn't quite decide whether to take his quietly spoken declaration as a promise or a threat.

TWO DAYS LATER, Savannah was in the tower room, enjoying the warmth of the fire as she stood in front of the window and watched Blake walk along the beach. Although she'd gotten into the habit of joining him on his frequent walks, this afternoon she'd begged off, pleading the feminine excuse of a headache. In truth, she needed some time alone. Time to try to unravel her tangled feelings about this frustratingly solitary man.

She wanted him. Desperately. Every morning, she would come down the stairs, walk into the kitchen where she'd find him reading the paper over his morning coffee and be hit by a stab of desire that could only be described as visceral.

During the day, she'd glance over to where he was working the Moviola editing machine, watch his strong hands turn the film wheels and grow warm as she remembered, in dazzling detail, exactly how those hands had felt on her body.

In the evening, as they sat in front of the fire in the tower room—immersed in mutual silence, the cat curled up between them on the sofa while Cujo offered random, pithy comments from his perch—she realized that she'd never felt so comfortable with anyone. And late at night, lying in her lonely antique bed, she'd rerun their lovemaking over and over again, like the flickering scenes from an erotic movie....

She watched him stop and pick something up from the damp gray sand, study it, then slip it into the pocket of his leather jacket. As if sensing her watching him, he looked up at the window and for a suspended moment, their gazes met and held. Then he continued down the beach.

Cujo left his perch and settled on her shoulder. No longer afraid of the gregarious, talkative bird, Savannah reached up and absently stroked his black feathers.

Blake was a puzzle inside an enigma. He was not an easy man to get to know. His reputation—of being cool, aloof, intensely private—was partly true. But she'd seen glimpses of another Blake Winters: a warm, caring man who could laugh—and love.

Savannah sighed. No, he wasn't an easy man to know, and he would be an even more difficult man to love. *If* she were in love with him. Which, of course, she wasn't.

"The lady doth protest too much."

Cujo tilted his head, studying her with his unblinking black eyes. Unnerved by the way the bird had hit just a little too close to home, Savannah felt a slight inner twinge.

BLAKE WASN'T SURPRISED when he looked up at the window and saw Savannah standing there. He'd felt her watching him. Somehow, during these past days, something indefinable had happened between them, allowing them to sense each other's thoughts and feelings. He had tried to come up with a time that had ever happened to him with any other person and came up blank. What he and Savannah shared was almost like a Vulcan mind-meld, he considered with a dry smile.

Analyzing emotions did not come easily to Blake; he had long ago accepted that about himself. In his more introspective moments he often thought that was why he was so drawn to making films. It allowed him to explore his own inner turmoil on that giant silver screen and later, when he slipped unnoticed into the back row of a theater and watched an audience respond to his vision, he was forced to consider that perhaps he wasn't as unique as he liked to think. Or as solitary.

Blake enjoyed living alone. At least, he had before Savannah Starr had taken hold of the orderly tapestry he'd woven of his life, plucked loose a few tidy threads, and changed everything. As he continued walking along the water's edge, it occurred to him that he enjoyed Savannah's company.

Which was totally unexpected. A reclusive man, Blake didn't like people invading his space, infiltrating his haven. But rather than being intrusive, Savannah's presence under his roof made him feel something dangerously close to contentment.

Something else had changed, as well. Although he still wanted her—painfully—during these past days, he'd found himself wanting her friendship, too. This was a subtle change in their relationship that he didn't quite understand and wasn't certain he cared for. But it was a fact—one he was going to have to face when their work together was done.

In the meantime, he was going to have to rely on his self-control to keep from dragging her off to bed at the slightest provocation. After a checkered youth that had included more fistfights than he cared to count, Blake had learned to harness his more primitive emotions with a strength others found discomfitting.

He'd been called, by both acquaintances and enemies, an unfeeling son of a bitch. During his marriage to Pamela, she had managed to come up with several even less-complimentary epithets.

None of the unflattering descriptions had bothered him. Blake had never cared what others thought of him. Or said about him. Until Savannah. She was the one woman he didn't want to think him cold or unfeeling—because she was the first woman he'd ever met who elicited pure emotion.

Looking out to sea, Blake brooded. Unfortunately, Savannah was also the one woman with whom he didn't dare lose control. The tide was coming in. A froth of icy water washed over his boots. As he turned back toward the house, Blake wondered when, exactly, his hard-won self-restraint had become a prison.

She was back at the synthesizer when Blake returned. Immersed in her work, she hadn't heard him come up the stairs. Taking advantage of the opportunity to watch her undetected, he leaned against the doorjamb, enjoying the view.

The synthesizer was capable of duplicating an amazing array of sounds and at the moment, Savannah was struggling with a passage of woodwinds. Her slender fingers moved over the keys again and again—sometimes changing a single note; at others, altering the time of a few bars or a phrase.

He understood her almost-compulsive need for precision. How many times had he labored over a scene or even a single line of dialogue? Blake decided that Savannah's refusal to accept less than perfection was something else they had in common.

If he was keeping score.

Which he wasn't.

The hell, he wasn't.

8

SAVANNAH WAS WORKING nearly around the clock. After taking a cryptic, strangely threatening message for Blake from the studio, she'd learned about his deadline dilemma and was determined that she not be the cause of him losing artistic control.

As the days passed, she also learned to find her way around the labyrinthine corridors of Blake's house with ease. Familiarity also brought comfort as she realized the house wasn't nearly as spooky as she'd first thought. Her attitude immediately changed, however, the morning Blake insisted on taking her down into the basement.

Descending the narrow, creaky wooden stairs into the lurking shadows, Savannah felt exactly like a heroine from some Gothic romance novel. Or from a Edgar Allan Poe story.

"Tell me again why I need to come down here," she complained. Something rustled in the corner. Savannah stifled a scream as a small gray field mouse scurried across the room.

Blake appeared not to notice. "So you can learn how the boiler works."

"I know all I need to know about the boiler. I turn on the tap and presto, hot water comes out. What else is there to know?"

"This, for one thing," he said, pointing to a complex assortment of gauges, handles and dials. "It's important to check the steam level every so often. If the pressure builds up and steam isn't released, this entire house could blow sky-high."

"Oh."

Savannah leaned closer. Perhaps he had a point, after all, she decided, as she watched him demonstrate the heating system that was a great deal more complicated than her own electric furnace. Actually, now that she thought about it, Savannah had never seen her furnace. It sat atop her roof, obediently blowing warm air whenever she flipped the switch.

Nothing about Blake Winters—his work, his inscrutable personality, even this house with its temperamental, turn-of-the-century boiler—was simple. But wasn't that partly why she found him so intriguing? she asked herself.

After Blake was convinced that Savannah knew how to operate the seemingly inexhaustible boiler, they went back upstairs to the studio where they were still working long after the sun had sunk into the sea.

Although she'd grown accustomed to having Blake watch her work, Savannah found herself growing more and more uncomfortable.

The scene she was scoring was a pivotal one: the first lovemaking scene between the bridegroom and his vampire bride. The couple was spending their honeymoon in a remote, Gothic hotel that was eerily similar to Blake's own home. Like Blake's, it was also perched precariously on a cliff overlooking a storm-tossed sea.

Instead of the customary klieg lights, Blake had lit the scene with dozens of flickering white candles that reminded Savannah of the beeswax ones in her own bedroom upstairs. A fire crackled in the stone fireplace while outside the leaded windows a storm raged. Thunder boomed and lightning flashed, intermittently bathing the room in a brilliant, stuttering white light.

The old-fashioned four-poster bed was draped in yards and yards of diaphanous white gauze. At the beginning of the scene, the camera captured only the shadows of the two lovers as they embraced, drew apart, then embraced again. The slow, soulful sound of a saxophone matched the rhythm of their movements.

Cut to a medium shot. The shadowy woman began undressing her new husband. She unbuttoned his white dress-shirt, flinging its ebony studs aside with sensual abandon. As she pressed her lips against each new bit of exposed flesh, her long hair, draped over his naked chest, shimmered in the candlelight like a platinum curtain.

The camera cut to the fire, over to the rain-lashed windows, and then slowly circled the room, taking in every exquisitely-styled detail: the wax dripping down the sides of the fat white candles, the cream satin high heels lying on the plank floor, a pair of diamond-and-pearl earrings discarded on the bedside table, the gossamer wedding veil abandoned on a gold satin chair, an open champagne bottle, the glittering chips of ice surrounding it melting in the silver bucket.

The camera continued toward the bed, past its billowy draperies, moving over the couple with the sensuality of a lover's caress. The woman left the plump feather mattress long enough to bend down and pull the high-necked, lacy confection of a wedding dress over her head. The gown fell to the floor in a billowy cloud of white European lace and seed pearls.

Beneath the dress, she was wearing a white merry-widow that plunged nearly to her navel while displaying full, firm breasts remarkable even by Hollywood standards. The snowy lace of the merrywidow was so sheer that it could have been spun from spiderwebs. A white lace string bikini, a matching garter belt and lace-topped white stockings completed her ensemble.

Along with, Savannah noticed, admiring Blake's unerring eye for detail, a strand of glowing white pearls.

The woman stood beside the bed for a long, silent moment, letting her husband drink in the provocative sight. Except for its color, there was nothing virginal about such wedding-night lingerie. As Savannah added some brass to the sax, she decided with a small, inward sigh, that this woman was probably every man's secret fantasy come to life.

The groom stared, spellbound. The music, like the woman herself, seemed to taunt him. Woodwinds flowed in and out of the melody, like the sound of a soft summer breeze blowing through the grass of a lush, flower-strewn meadow.

Her flesh gleamed like warm satin in the candlelight; as the groom reached out to touch it, something dangerous flickered in her silvery eyes—something as compelling as it was frightening. The all-seeing eye of Blake's camera captured both the man's fear and his unwilling fascination before returning to the woman's face. Her eyes had turned as hard as silver dollars, but her enticing smile, and the way her hands moved invitingly over her own curves, drew him nearer.

Outside the honeymoon suite, a full moon rose in a midnight-black sky. Inside, the sexual tension was building. Savannah reminded herself that these were only actors playing their parts. They were paid to pretend passion. Soon Blake would yell, "Cut!" the magic would disappear and everyone would go home. But even as she told herself that, she found her own body warming, responding to the sensual crescendo Blake had so brilliantly orchestrated.

Even as she fought against the feelings the lushly erotic scene evoked, even as she struggled to keep her mind on the music, Savannah couldn't help wondering if this was how Pamela had appeared to Blake on their wedding night. And if so, how horribly she must pale in comparison.

Blake, who had begun watching the scene with a director's hypercritical eye, realized he'd made a fatal mistake in viewing this particular scene with Savannah. As he watched the actress's silvery blond hair drape across the man's chest, all he could think about was how Savannah's hair had felt like silk against his skin. And when the woman's lips skimmed down the actor's chest, the memory of Savannah's tender kisses made his own flesh burn.

And when the actress took off her wedding dress, displaying herself with arrogant female pride, Blake remembered Savannah's endearing and entirely misplaced fear that he'd find her body unattractive.

Compared to the frothy white lingerie worn by the actress in the wedding-night scene, Savannah's underwear—plain white cotton and as starkly utilitarian as a nun's—had been an admitted surprise. Blake would have expected a woman of Savannah's intensely passionate nature to have been wearing satin and lace. Black, perhaps. Or even red.

Puzzled at first, Blake had since decided that believing her body to be flawed, Savannah had taken to wearing the decidedly unsexy lingerie in an attempt to suppress her sexuality.

He smiled. She might as well try to stop the tide from rising and ebbing. Or the sun from coming up each morning. Because the truth of the matter was that Savannah Starr was the most passionate woman he'd ever known. He couldn't remember when he'd wanted a woman more than Savannah. He couldn't remember when he'd *needed* a woman more.

His body stirred, painfully reminding him that it had been much too long since he'd held her in his arms; since he'd watched her dark eyes widen in amazement as he took them both over the edge.

The images continued to flicker on the screen. Savannah's body ached as she watched the man's strong dark hands move over the woman's glistening flesh. Just the memory of Blake's hand touching her in that very same way made her own skin grow hot and sensitized.

The couple lying amid the love-tangled sheets was naked now. The woman was clad only in her pearls and as she drew him down on top of her—his dark male flesh against her ivory female flesh—she draped the necklace over his head, as well, holding him to her with the gleaming strand of beads.

Savannah glanced over at Blake, saw his faint smile and wondered at its cause. Was he remembering Pamela? Was he remembering what it had been like to make love to her perfect body?

The mood was intensifying. Savannah's fingers trembled on the synthesizer keyboard; the music swelled. On the screen a log collapsed in the fire, sending forth a flare of orange sparks. The wind howled at the windows like a lost spirit, a ghostly white ring encircled the cold pale moon.

The groom was lost in an overwhelming passion. So much so that he didn't notice the change in his new bride. He didn't notice the way her silver eyes changed to flame; he didn't see the needle-sharp fangs appear from between her ruby-red lips.

Savannah introduced a clash of percussion as the woman buried those sharp white fangs deep into the mahogany flesh of her husband's neck.

The milky pearls broke, scattering over the bed, over the floor. Fade to black.

"Wow." Exhausted, Savannah slumped back in the chair and ran her hands through her hair. She was nervous. Confused.

"Wow, indeed," Blake agreed numbly. "Once the ratings board sees what you've done to that scene, we'll be lucky if we can pull a NC-17."

"What *I* did to the scene?"

Savannah spun around in her chair and made the mistake of looking directly into his eyes. The banked fires smoldering in those depths told her that she hadn't been the only one unduly influenced by the highly charged scene. "You're the director, Blake."

In an effort to break away from his steady, heated gaze, she jumped out of her chair and went over to the window, where she stood looking over the moon-gilded sea. "You're also the producer and the writer," she reminded him needlessly. "All I did was add some music."

"You made that scene come alive," he argued. "I can't remember when I've had a song go straight to my blood like that." Blake found himself wanting everything that her music had hinted at. The heat. The passion. God help him, even the madness.

"The intensity was already there. I simply tried to echo the mood you'd created."

His fingers practically itched with the need to touch her. "Which you did. Brilliantly."

"Thank you."

Having already determined that Blake Winters was a perfectionist, Savannah knew that such rare words of praise should bring pleasure. And they probably would, she decided, as soon as her mind started working properly again. At the moment, that familiar, warm, giddy feeling was surging through her, leaving her weak.

Blake swore softly. "I give up." He stood and crossed the room to stand behind her. "I promised I wouldn't force you into my bed, Savannah. And I meant it."

Taking hold of her shoulders he gently turned her around to face him. A myriad of emotions were swirling in her eyes—confusion, apprehension, desire. Blake concentrated on the desire. "But patience has never been my long suit and I think I'll go mad if I have to wait for you any longer."

She pressed her hand against his chest. His heartbeat was slow and steady. But strong. "We agreed to keep things strictly business."

"That was your idea," Blake reminded her. "Right now, all I want to do is make love to you. And to sleep with you in my bed. All night long. Then, tomorrow morning we can get back to business."

"What if I don't want that?" Savannah was appalled by the lack of conviction in her voice.

"Is that a hypothetical question?" He drew her closer.

As his jeans-clad thighs pressed against hers, as she felt the heat radiating from his body, sensations surrounded Savannah. Like morning fog they swirled around her, inside her—passion, desire, need—until they merged with the most powerful, the most dangerous of all emotions: love.

"You're only responding to the moment," she managed thickly. She couldn't get her breath. The air in the room had turned hot and sultry—just as she'd imagined it had been in Blake's powerfully erotic scene. "To the movie."

"Wrong." His hand moved slowly up her back, his fingers spreading to tangle in her hair. "I'm responding to you."

She wanted to believe it. Lord, how she longed to believe that she could create that hot, dangerous passion in his eyes! But dual images flashed treacherously through her mind.

The first was of her breathtakingly gorgeous mother, dressed in a cream silk kimono, seated at her dressing table, rubbing scented French cream into her face. "A woman's beauty is her most important asset," Melanie Raine was saying with unwavering conviction. "Never forget, Savannah, dear, without beauty, a woman is nothing."

The second disturbing image that flashed in front of Savannah's mind's eye was of newlywed Pamela Winters, her wet white swimming suit made nearly transparent as she frolicked playfully in the impossibly blue waters of a hidden Maui lagoon. A second, more intimate shot had shown the honeymoon couple making love on the beach. From a discreet distance, of course. The photos, which had been taken on Pamela and Blake's honeymoon by an enterprising room-service waiter, had appeared on the covers of supermarket tabloids all over the country.

"The actress in *Unholy Matrimony* looks just like your wife," Savannah said.

"So?" He ran the back of his hand down the side of her face. Last night, when he'd taken clean towels into her bathroom, he couldn't help noticing that Savannah eschewed the lotions and creams that most women seemed addicted to. And rightly so. Her skin was as soft and delicate as the inside of a rose petal. He could spend the rest of his life just touching it. Tasting it.

"So, that was an incredibly sensual scene," Savannah argued weakly. The light touch of his hand on her skin was making her dizzy. "It would be natural for you to react to lingering sexual feelings for Pamela—to the fantasy of the woman you thought you were marrying."

If Savannah's expression hadn't been so serious, if he hadn't seen the unwilling vulnerability in her eyes, Blake would have laughed. Instead, he framed her face with his palms, stunned to find that his own hands were no longer steady.

"Believe me, Savannah, I could never confuse you with my former wife. Despite all outward appearances to the contrary, Pamela was ice." He let his gaze wander over her still-exquisite face. "You, on the other hand, are fire. And the fantasy I'm responding to revolves around you."

He traced her top lip with his thumbnail. "The way you feel in my arms when we're making love. The incredible, terrifying way you make me feel."

He was looking at her as if she were the only woman he had ever seen—had ever wanted, or would ever want. Making her decision, Savannah ran her fingers over the firm bones of his face, over his dark skin roughened by a day's growth of beard.

"Only with you," she whispered, the wonder of her admission shimmering in her soft tone. "It's only that way with you."

Twining her arms around his neck, Savannah lifted her parted lips to his and surrendered to the fantasy.

SAVANNAH FELT the light kiss on her shoulder and snuggled against Blake, murmuring soft, inarticulate sounds of pleasure. Outside his bedroom window, she could hear pigeons cooing, signaling the beginning of a new day. But she was in no hurry to get up. Indeed, she thought she could quite happily spend the rest of her life basking in this strange feeling of warmth, security and excitement.

Last night had been like a dream. Or something out of a midnight fantasy. Something about Blake had her giving more than she'd ever given to any other man. Something about him had her wanting from him more than any man had ever given her. She sighed as his hand moved slowly down her side, settling on her hip. *Definitely a fantasy,* she decided.

But now it was morning. And fantasies, like dreams, belonged to the night.

She opened her eyes and looked into Blake's.

"What time is it?"

"Early." He combed a hand through her tangled hair and left it resting on her cheek.

His gaze was warm, his touch unnervingly possessive. Savannah was not accustomed to waking up with any man, let alone one as sexually disheveled as Blake was in the morning. Feeling ridiculously self-conscious, she tightened her fingers around the sheet and tugged it higher.

"I suppose we'd better get to work." She glanced around Blake's room for her clothes, finally remembering that she hadn't been wearing any when he'd finally carried her downstairs to his bed.

Her fingers were moving restlessly on the sheet. Blake closed his hands over them. "We've plenty of time."

"But if the film isn't scored on time, the studio will take it away from you."

Blake was beginning to wish Savannah had never found out about his little battle of wills with the studio heads. Especially since he could think of far more appealing ways to spend this morning.

"Don't worry. We're ahead of schedule." He brushed his lips up her cheek. "We still have more than a week, and all you have left to write is the title song."

It was hard to think when he was causing such havoc to her senses. "Please, Blake—" When he tugged at the sheet, she clutched tighter.

"It's a little late to be nervous around me, sweetheart."

Color flooded into her cheeks. "I'm not nervous."

Another lie. Savannah's soft, wide eyes and tender mouth were the kind that could encourage a man to forget that there was such a thing as feminine guile. If he were careless. Or foolish. But Blake was not a careless or foolish man. Nor was he a man to resist a challenge.

"Yes, you are." His hand slipped beneath the sheet to cup her breast. "Of course," he said, trailing his hand down her rib cage, "I suppose I could take that as a compliment."

Blake heard Savannah suck in her breath as his fingers trailed over her stomach. He felt her stiffen and ignored it. "I think I rather like knowing that you haven't begun to take me for granted."

A thousand pulses were humming just beneath her skin. The need to make love with Blake warred with Savannah's fear of having him see her scarred body in the unforgiving light of day.

"Blake—"

Was it her nerves he was trying to soothe? Blake wondered. Or his? Unwilling to consider that little problem right now, he forestalled Savannah's planned argument by closing his mouth over hers.

He kissed her—not with the heated passion of the night before, but with the slow, warm affection of a longtime lover. Savannah, who'd been braced for heat and flames found herself falling under the spell of the unbearably tender kiss.

He murmured her name. Savannah answered with a soft, yielding sigh. There was sweetness. Slow, savoring, sensual sweetness. Savannah had never known anything like it. Music was playing inside her head; it flowed through her, impossibly happy, yet achingly sad.

And then, suddenly, the music stopped.

"Damn." Blake glared at the ringing telephone beside his bed. He wanted to ignore it. But he couldn't. Not when it could be the police calling with news of Larsen.

He scooped up the receiver with a muffled curse. "Winters. Oh. Sorry, I was expecting someone else." He exchanged a glance with Savannah. "Sure. She's right here." He handed the receiver to her. "It's your father."

He'd been on tour; she hadn't talked to him for months. Sitting up, Savannah pulled the sheet up to her chin. Blake arched a eyebrow at her modesty; Savannah ignored it.

"Hello, Pop."

"What in the bloody 'ell is a daughter of mine doin' shacked up with a crazy bloke like Blake Winters?" Reggie Starr demanded in the deep, gravelly voice that had made all the girls at Liverpool's Quarry Bank High School—the very same school that had given the world

Paul McCartney and John Lennon—go weak in the knees. After thirty years, that inimitable voice could still make young girls scream and their mothers swoon.

Trust her father to get right to the point. "Does this mean you've changed your views on free love?"

"In case you haven't heard, luv, the sexual revolution is over."

"Now that you mention it, I believe I did hear rumors of its demise," Savannah said easily. "But you don't have to worry about me. Somehow, when I wasn't looking, the sexual revolution passed me by."

"Awright then. I'm glad to hear it."

This from the man whose alleged sexual exploits had achieved legendary proportions, Savannah thought with a smile. In fact, if even half of what had been reported in *Rolling Stone* magazine was true, Reggie Starr was one of rock's busiest—and potentially exhausted—singers.

"So what are you doin' hiding away in Mendocino with Hollywood's infamous lone wolf?" Reggie asked.

"We're working together. I'm scoring Blake's new film." She exchanged a soft smile with Blake. "It's a wonderful opportunity."

"That's the same thing Justin said when I rung him up this morning. In fact, 'e says that you're both probably goin' to get Oscars. I'm glad you're finally using some of the talents you inherited from your old man... So, you're really not sleepin' with Winters?"

"I really don't think that's any of your business."

There was a long thoughtful silence. "Well, I suppose it's only natural," he decided. "Working as close together as you are, and all."

Before Savannah could respond to that, he dropped his bombshell. "The reason I'm calling, Savannah, luv, is to invite you to the wedding."

"Wedding? You're getting married? Again?"

"Ain't that a bleedin' stunner?" Reggie asked with a laugh. "I'm still pinchin' myself in case I'm dreamin'. I met Audrey backstage at a concert in Chicago last month, and fell head over arse in love. But I never thought I could convince her to say yes."

Savannah was not all that surprised. His last marriage—to a groupie five years younger than Savannah—hadn't lasted long enough for the ink to dry on the marriage license. After four stormy weeks, the bride had walked, carrying with her the Louis Vuitton luggage Reggie had bought her for a wedding present, a check for a million pounds, and a lucrative contract with a Fleet Street publisher for an unauthorized biography of one of rock and roll's most colorful bad boys.

"I'm happy for you, Dad."

"Wait till you meet her, Savannah." He appeared not to hear the lack of enthusiasm in his daughter's tone. "She's a special lady." That's exactly what he'd said about the groupie, Savannah recalled.

"When is the wedding?"

"Five o'clock tomorrow afternoon."

"Tomorrow? So soon?"

"Sorry to spring it on you, luv, but I want to get my ring on her finger before she wises up and changes her mind. But we're just down the coast, at the San Francisco Fairmont. If you leave right now, we'll have lots of time for you and Audrey and Winters and I to get acquainted."

The idea of Blake and her father in the same room was overwhelming. Although they were both remarkably talented, they couldn't have been more opposite. They were, Savannah considered, like two sides of a coin. Everything Reggie felt was on the surface, out in the open for the world to see. Whereas Blake kept everything tightly bottled up inside.

"But I don't have anything with me that's even remotely suitable for a wedding."

"Don't worry about it. You and Audrey can go shopping after your lunch tomorrow."

Savannah wondered idly about Audrey's taste in clothes. The groupie had favored spandex and leather. "Our lunch?"

"It was Audrey's idea," Reggie revealed. "She thought the two women in my life should get better acquainted. Meanwhile, I can check out Winters and make sure the bloke's good enough for you."

Savannah turned away from Blake. "Please, Dad," she whispered into the receiver, "I have to work with Blake. Promise you won't do anything to embarrass me."

"Me? Embarrass my favorite girl?"

Reggie sounded shocked that she'd even suggest such a thing. Savannah decided not to mention the time, a year after her parents' divorce, when he'd flown her to New York City for the holidays. They'd spent the morning skating on the Rockefeller Center ice rink. Then, after lunch at the Russian Tea Room, he'd taken her shopping at F.A.O. Schwarz, where he'd bought her more dolls and stuffed animals than any eight-year-old girl could ever play with.

That evening, they'd attended the Radio City Music Hall Christmas show. Savannah wore the red velvet Christmas dress her mother had purchased for the occasion; Reggie—always the rebel—had been clad in black T-shirt, tight leather pants and silver-toed cowboy boots.

Granted, she'd had a memorable day. But her father had had an even more memorable night when he and one of the long-legged Rockettes had decided to go skinny dipping in the Pulitzer fountain outside the Plaza Hotel.

Savannah shook her head in mute frustration. "Promise me."

"Awright," Reggie agreed with a huff. "I promise, on my word of honor, as a gent, not to embarrass my daughter with her fella. How's that?"

Savannah decided that there was no point in insisting that Blake wasn't her fellow. "Thank you," she said instead. "And now, I'd better go pack. See you in a bit." Exchanging goodbyes, she hung up the phone.

"You didn't sound exactly thrilled by your father's news," Blake observed.

She shrugged. "Since it's his sixth marriage, I suppose I should be used to it by now. I want him to be happy. Really, I do, but..." Her voice drifted off. "There's something else."

"What?"

"He asked about you. Us."

"So I gathered. I thought you handled it admirably."

"It isn't going to be enough," Savannah warned. "He wants me to bring you to San Francisco for the wedding."

"Terrific. I rather like the idea of making love to you in one of the most romantic cities in the world."

"You don't understand what you're getting into." Savannah dragged her hand through her hair. "I know it sounds ridiculous, given his own outrageous lifestyle, but my father's always been unreasonably protective of me."

"I'd say that's understandable," Blake said mildly.

"But Reggie was that way even before Jerry. He was a terror when I was in high school and college. He never thought any of the boys I dated were good enough for me."

"I suppose every man feels that way," Blake considered, "when he has to face the idea of giving away his daughter."

"Perhaps." Savannah sounded unconvinced. "Whatever the reason, I just know that he's going to grill you while I'm off having lunch with my new stepmother."

"Is that all that's bothering you?" Worry lines were etched into her forehead. Blake smoothed them away with his fingertip. "Don't worry about me. I can handle your father, Savannah."

"It's obvious that you haven't met my father," Savannah muttered. "There's another thing. The hotel is undoubtedly teeming with his fans. And reporters."

"So?"

"So, how are we going to explain us being there together?"

"Simple. We're working together. End of story."

End of story. Savannah reminded herself that she'd entered into this affair with her eyes wide open. Blake hadn't promised her any happily-ever-afters. Nor had she asked for any. But somehow, hearing it stated so coldly made her relationship with Blake seem so . . . tawdry. Rising from the bed, she wrapped the sheet toga-style around her naked body.

"I'd better take a shower."

The sensual mood had passed. Blake tried to console himself with the thought that there would be others. "Need any help with that hard-to-reach spot in the middle of your back?"

"That sounds very nice," she said with a stiffly formal politeness that belied the lusty way they'd spent the night. "But we don't have much time."

She wanted him. But she was afraid of him. Blake saw both things clearly. "Whatever you say."

Something suddenly occurred to her. "What are we going to do with Cujo? And the cat?"

Blake shrugged. "Sam's due back tomorrow. We can drop Cujo off at his place. As for the cat, in case you hadn't noticed, he comes and goes as he pleases."

She had. But it hadn't registered. "But how does he get in and out of the house?"

"This place was used for rum-running during Prohibition," Blake divulged. "There are a lot of secret passages. Obviously, the cat's located one of them."

"Oh." Something else occurred to her. Something definitely unpalatable. All the color drained from her face. "If there are ways into the house—"

His fingers tightened around her upper arms and he shook her gently. "Larsen's not going to hurt you, Savannah. He hasn't any way of knowing you're here."

"But—"

"I promise the bastard won't get anywhere near you."

Something in his eyes made Savannah believe him—an unsettling possessiveness that she'd have to think about later. "I'd better get dressed," she said, anxious to escape his intense gaze.

Blake let her go, but he stood where he was, beside the bed, thinking, long after he'd heard the door close down the hallway.

Twenty minutes later, Savannah had showered and dressed and was in the process of packing.

"Another stepmother," she muttered as she took a pair of white cotton briefs out of the bureau and tossed them into her suitcase. Her aversion to meeting the latest in her father's long line of women overrode her uneasiness concerning Blake.

"Just what I always wanted. One of these days we should all get together and hold a reunion."

9

THE FAIRMONT HOTEL crowned Nob Hill like a jewel.

"You're realize that you're acting as if you're going to a public hanging," Blake said as he pulled the car beneath the wide porte cochere. The closer they'd gotten to the city, the quieter she'd become; she hadn't said a word for the past twenty minutes.

Savannah sighed. "I know. And I also know that if I'm going to insist that my life is none of my father's business, then I should just decide to live and let live." She shook her head in mute frustration. "It's just that all my life, all I ever really wanted was a normal family."

Blake chuckled at that, but the sound held no humor. "Join the club. But the truth is the Cleavers were simply one in a long line of Hollywood illusions." He touched her hair. "Perhaps the thing to do is to make your own family."

It was only a hand to her hair. Certainly not an earthshakingly intimate gesture. But that seemingly casual touch, along with the warmth of his gaze, made her tremble.

Before she could think up an answer, a liveried doorman, clad in a black uniform with broad red epaulets and shiny brass buttons, opened the passenger door and Savannah had no choice but to accompany Blake into the hotel.

The lobby was richly decorated with marble pillars and a gilt-framed ceiling that recalled San Francisco's golden era. They were making their way across the plush black-and-burgundy carpeting when a familiar face appeared in front of them.

"Justin!"

The slight frown on Savannah's face was replaced with a dazzling smile that rivaled the glow from the crystal chandeliers overhead. Flinging her arms around his neck, she went up on her toes to kiss the older man's tanned cheek. "I didn't expect to see you here."

"You don't think I'd miss one of your father's weddings, do you?" the agent said. "I have, after all, served as best man at all the others."

He glanced over the top of Savannah's dark head. "Hello, Blake." If he was surprised to see his longtime client with Savannah, he didn't show it.

Blake had been standing by quietly, watching the way Savannah had reacted to Justin Peters's unexpected appearance.

The reserve she normally wore like a protective cloak had fallen away and she was behaving with a free-spirited spontaneity he'd only experienced while they were making love. Blake found himself wishing they could spend all their time in bed.

"Hello, Justin." A man was losing his grip when he became jealous of his best—and perhaps only—friend. Blake knew it. But that didn't stop him from wanting to pry Justin's hand off Savannah's hip.

The older man lifted an eyebrow at Blake's curt tone. "It's good to see you. How's the work going?"

"Very well," Blake answered. "Savannah's an incredible talent."

"It's Blake who's talented," Savannah quickly said. "If my score is any good, it's only because his marvelous scenes provided such inspiration."

Justin's gaze went from Blake to Savannah and back to Blake again. "Sounds like a mutual-admiration society. Although I hate to take credit for others' abilities, I suspected all along that my two favorite clients would hit it off."

Blake was suspicious, but if the agent had been involved in a little underhanded matchmaking, he wasn't saying. "Why don't you two go up upstairs and unpack?" Justin suggested, handing them a key. "Then you can join your father and Audrey. Reggie's hiding away in his suite. So far, no one knows he's in town."

Which was lucky, Savannah considered as she accompanied Blake upstairs in the elevator. Because whatever her relationship with Blake—and after last night, she could no longer continue to deny that they did, indeed, have some sort of relationship—it was too new, too fragile, to be exposed to the savage scrutiny of the press.

Her father had booked them into the Ambassador Suite. With his usual flair, along with the basket of fruit and cheeses provided by the hotel, Reggie had arranged for a magnum of champagne. Beside it, a silver bowl of gleaming dark caviar was nestled in a bed of sparkling ice.

"All the comforts of home," Blake murmured.

"My father's inordinately fond of grand gestures," Savannah said. "He can't seem to get over having grown up poor, so he constantly surrounds himself with all the trappings of wealth."

"I suppose I can understand that," Blake said. Wasn't it one of the reasons he continued to squeeze fresh orange juice every morning? To keep the fantasy alive— and the hounds of his own impoverished past at bay?

"Unfortunately, he always forgets that I hate caviar."

"You, too?" Another thing they had in common. After last night, Blake had given up trying to convince himself that he wasn't keeping score.

Savannah laughed. "My father categorically refuses to believe that I'd rather have a hot dog."

"With relish and mustard. At the ballpark," Blake said. "Watching the Giants beat the Dodgers."

"Watching the Dodgers beat the Giants," Savannah corrected. Crossing the room, she pulled the heavy blackout draperies closed, blocking out the sun and throwing the room into shadow.

Blake stared at her. "Good Lord, don't tell me you're a Dodgers fan."

She crossed her arms over her chest and came to stand in front of him. "True-blue. And surely you aren't really a Giants fan?"

"Dyed-in-the-wool." Blake shook his head. "Damn. I guess this relationship is doomed."

"It appears so." Savannah sighed and ran her hands up his chambray shirtfront to his throat. "But perhaps there is a solution to our little problem."

"What's that?"

She could hear the desire in his rough tone. Thrilled that she could affect Blake with such a simple touch, Savannah toyed with the top button of his shirt.

"Perhaps," she suggested silkily, freeing the button while watching his eyes, "we could stick to basketball games." She loosened the second button. Then the third. "How do you feel about the Lakers?"

The touch of her hand made Blake's flesh burn, his head swim. He'd lost the power to control his thoughts. His body. His pulse.

"I love 'em," he managed.

Their mouths met and conversation ceased, and was replaced by soft sighs and husky moans as they rocketed into the mist.

AUDREY LYNDON WAS a revelation. Tall and elegant, with silver hair that had been swept back into a French roll, dressed in a classic Chanel suit and a single strand of very good pearls, she was definitely older than Savannah. In fact, a stunned Savannah considered, it was possible that Audrey was actually as old as Reggie.

They had met, as Reggie had told Savannah on the phone, after last month's show in Chicago. But she wasn't really a groupie, Audrey assured Savannah with a smile. In fact, she had been only vaguely aware of Reggie Starr's music and had never bought an album. Rather, in addition to being first cellist for the San Francisco Symphony, she also served as the director of a music program for mentally-challenged teenagers.

Since her kids all idolized Reggie Starr, Audrey had flown to Chicago, where he was performing, to ask him to headline a benefit talent-show designed to raise much-needed funds for her pet program.

"She was the most persuasive woman I've ever met," Reggie told Savannah and Blake during dinner. "By the time she was five minutes into her spiel, I would've done anything she asked. By the time she was finished, I knew she was going to marry me."

"Fast work on both your parts," Blake said.

Savannah watched as Audrey reached over and covered Reggie's hand with her own beringed one. A shimmering diamond covered the ring finger of her left hand. Reggie, true to form, had bought the largest piece of crystallized carbon Cartier had had in stock.

"Reggie can be quite persuasive, himself," Audrey said with an indulgent, loving smile.

"When it's somethin'—or someone—I want," Reggie agreed, unknowingly echoing Blake's words as he answered his fiancée's smile with a boyish one of his own.

As the evening progressed, Savannah came to the conclusion that Audrey was definitely a woman of vast talents. Including being a magician. Somehow, without so much as a whip or a chair, she managed to keep Reggie Starr behaving like a perfect gentleman.

"He has to be under some sort of spell," Savannah told Blake when they were alone in their hotel room. "I've never seen my father act so . . . so . . ." She was at an absolute loss for words.

"Normal?" Blake suggested.

"Exactly. If I didn't know better, I'd say that Audrey is a pod person and has gotten rid of the real Reggie Starr—Britain's bad boy of rock and roll—and replaced him with this friendly, funny, balding, almost respectable middle-aged man. And did you notice his suit?"

"Savile Row."

"My father has never worn a suit in his life. Unless you count the black leather tuxedo he wore to last year's Grammy Awards. And his earring's gone."

"Love can do funny things to a man," Blake said.

"I suppose."

If she'd been paying more attention, Savannah would have heard the personal admission in Blake's tone. But she was thinking about her father's missing earring. He'd worn the gleaming gold stud for as long as she'd known him. Once he'd told her that it had belonged to her mother. She'd been wearing a pair of them the night they'd met—the night Melanie Raine's studio had arranged for the brash young Liverpudlian rock singer to accompany the rising star to the premier of her new movie. The night that Savannah had been conceived.

Blake was right. Love did funny things to people. It made them fight. It made them jealous. It made them weak, and sometimes, it made them murderous. From what she'd seen of love, Savannah didn't want any part of it.

"I just want him to be happy," she said softly.

"Then you don't have to worry," Blake said. "Because it's obvious that your father is a very happy man, these days." He began unfastening the row of tiny gold buttons that ran down the front of her black dinner dress. "I have a proposition for you."

Savannah reached over and switched off the light. "Yes," she said as he pushed the dress off her shoulders. It slid to the carpet.

"You don't even know what I was going to suggest."

She stepped out of the dress. "Try me."

"I was thinking that instead of going back right after the wedding tomorrow, we spend another night."

"I think that's an absolutely wonderful idea." His shirt joined her dress. "So did the hotel manager when I called down and told him that we'd be keeping the room for another day."

Savannah was laughing when he pulled her down onto the bed.

"GOOD MORNING." The mellow morning sunshine was filtering through a slit in the draperies. Blake shifted on the bed to draw Savannah closer. "You are exquisite."

His fingers were gently stroking her breast. She quickly pulled the sheet up to her shoulders. "You're not so bad yourself."

He lifted her hand to his lips. "I only wish I could figure out a way to keep you in my bed like this all the time."

The words were frighteningly familiar. Savannah stiffened in his arms and pulled her hand away. "I don't think that would be a very good idea."

Damn. What had he been thinking of? "Savannah." He ran his hand helplessly over her hair. "I'm sorry. I didn't mean it the way it sounded."

"I know." She sighed and rested her cheek on his chest. "You could never be like Jerry. I realize that. But sometimes old instincts die hard."

That he could understand. Last night, as he watched Reggie Starr bask in the glow of newly discovered love, Blake wondered grimly if he'd looked as stupidly love-struck the night before his marriage to Pamela, and had come to the reluctant conclusion that he probably had. The difference was that Audrey seemed to honestly love Reggie in spite of what he did for a living, while Pamela had only pretended to love him because of his career.

"Ghosts." Savannah lifted her head to look at him, her eyes brimming with understanding. "We all have them. And sometimes they refuse to stay locked away in their closets."

Two weeks ago, Savannah Starr had been nothing but a midnight fantasy. Now she was the single most important thing in his life. It couldn't be love. Oh, he loved working with her, he loved laughing with her, he loved walking along the beach with her and he definitely loved making love with her. But love?

Yes. Love. The knowledge, when it came, was not particularly welcome. He'd always considered falling in love to be a dangerous, foolish misstep, like taking a nosedive off the cliff behind his house. Well, that's exactly what had happened. He'd taken a nosedive, all right. Right into something he still wasn't sure he wanted.

"Ghosts," he repeated thoughtfully, wondering if Savannah could read all his thoughts. Or just the negative ones concerning Pamela. "I don't suppose you'd happen to know a good exorcist?"

Savannah smiled. "Not really. But perhaps," she suggested, pulling the sheet over both their heads, "if we put all of our positive energy together and concentrated really hard—"

"I knew you were an intelligent woman." A small, surprised gasp of pleasure escaped Savannah's lips as Blake slipped into her. Their hands linked, their lips met. And the ghosts vanished.

LATER, DURING A PRIVATE lunch with Reggie in his hotel suite, Blake discovered the Savannah wasn't kidding about her father's tendency for cross-examination.

"Those rumors," Reggie said, "the ones about you tryin' to kill your wife, I want you to know that I never believed them."

"I'm glad to hear that," Blake said dryly.

"Although thinkin' back on a couple of my own ex-wives, I can understand why you'd want to," Reggie allowed. "So, what are your intentions concerning my daughter?" he asked, eyeing Blake over the icy rim of his beer mug.

Blake took a drink of his own beer. "I like a man who gets straight to the point."

"When Savannah got mixed up with that Larsen bastard, I told myself that she was a grown woman," Reggie revealed. "Capable of makin' her own choices." His lips thinned and something that looked like a cross between pain and recrimination moved like a shadow across his face.

"I'm a man who learns from his mistakes, Winters, and the good Lord knows, I've made more than my share. But I won't make that same error concerning my daughter ever again. So, I'm askin' you again, what the flamin' 'ell are your intentions?"

Blake felt like suggesting that Reggie's own romantic track record made him an unlikely choice to control Savannah's personal life. He also found the entire conversation outrageously Victorian. But he could tell that while Reggie Starr hadn't been a perfect father figure for his daughter, he did love her. Which was one thing they shared.

"I love Savannah. And I'm going to marry her." As he heard the words leave his mouth, Blake was every bit as surprised to be saying them as Reggie seemed to be, hearing them.

"Talk about gettin' right to the bloody point," Reggie muttered, taking another long drink of beer. "Does Savannah know about this?"

"No."

Reggie appeared to mull that over. "She's not at all like her mother. Or me. With Melanie and I, what you see is what you get. Savannah was always more private. She tends to hold her feelings in. Sometimes too much, if you ask me."

"I know," Blake answered. "We have that in common."

"I suppose you do." Reggie studied Blake, looking far more like a concerned father than an international rock legend. "Her mother put some funny ideas in her head. Ideas about a woman not bein' worth anything if she isn't beauty-queen beautiful. All the time... That's why Melanie killed herself. Because she couldn't stand the idea of not being perfect."

He rubbed his hand over his face in a weary way that made Blake wonder if he was remembering how it felt to fall in love with a woman who possessed such a tragic flaw.

"I'm not saying Savannah would ever kill herself," Reggie insisted. "She's too strong for that. But I think, when she looks in the mirror, her scars look a lot worse to her than they do to the rest of us."

"I think they do," Blake concurred. Except for that first time, when she'd reluctantly allowed him to view her scars in the firelight, Savannah had insisted on making love in the dark. Or like this morning, under the covers. "But healing takes time. Especially emotional healing."

Reggie gave him an intense, judicial look. "I imagine you'd know a bit about that yourself."

"I do." Blake met the older man's probing eyes with a direct gaze of his own. "Your daughter's been good for me. I'm not going to lie and say that I wanted to get involved with her, because I damn well didn't. But I fell in love with her—the gorgeous, generous, talented woman she is inside—and if it takes me the rest of my life, I'm going to make her learn to trust enough to fall in love with me."

Reggie nodded, appearing convinced of Blake's sincerity. "If you want my opinion, Winters, I'd say you're halfway there." He grinned, and the cheeky rock singer was back. "I think I'll get the kid a set of drums."

"Kid?"

"My grandchild," Reggie explained guilelessly. "The family never has had a drummer. I like the idea of goin' out on the road with the little nipper. Savannah could write the songs, I'd sing 'em, and the boy could rip away at the percussion. Just think, three generations of Starrs all in the business at the same time."

"Just think," Blake murmured, deciding that this was one more little news flash that he was going to keep from Savannah.

SAN FRANCISCO'S temperamental spring weather cooperated beautifully for the outdoor wedding.

"I can't believe it," Savannah said on the way to Golden Gate Park. She was sitting in the back of a limousine with her father, Audrey, Justin and Blake. "Here we are, minutes away from pulling off the celebrity wedding of the year, and there aren't any hordes of screaming fans, autograph seekers, paparazzi, or helicopters flying overhead."

"That's because your old man used his noodle," Reggie said, handing her a folded newspaper.

Savannah stared in wonder at the supermarket tabloid. The cover featured a picture of her father, skiing in Gstaad with a blond beauty reported to be the unmarried daughter of the prince of Montacroix.

"I know they're not above putting people's heads on other people's bodies," she said. "But how—"

"I hired a bloke from one of those talent agencies specializing in celebrity lookalikes," Reggie informed her. "The guy's bloody amazing. He's almost a dead ringer. 'Cept I'm better-looking, of course."

"Your father's modesty was one of the reasons I fell in love with him," Audrey murmured with an indulgent smile.

"Hey, it was a right brilliant idea," Reggie said smugly. "As we speak, the entire bleedin' pack of Fleet

Street cannibals have followed my double to Gstaad, where, with any luck, they are freezin' their arses blue following the pair of lovers around in the snow all day."

Audrey patted his cheek. "It truly was a most brilliant plan, darling."

"Absolutely," the other three members of the wedding party agreed in unison.

Once a region of worthless sand dunes, Golden Gate Park's rolling hills had been transformed into over one thousand acres of gardens, lawns and forests. Audrey and Reggie had chosen the Japanese Tea Garden for their wedding, and there, amid the carp-filled ponds, arched footbridges, blooming cherry trees and bonsai gardens, Savannah held hands with Blake and watched her father and his new bride exchange vows.

Audrey was, as all brides should be, lovely in a tealength dress of rose silk. Reggie, clad in a dark blue suit—another one, Savannah realized with amazement—was his usual cocky self, although Savannah thought that he looked a trifle pale beneath his Mediterranean tan. And his voice, when he promised to love and honor Audrey, lacked its usual strong timbre.

Following the brief ceremony, they celebrated with a wedding supper in a private dining room at the hotel. Later that evening, Justin returned to Los Angeles and Reggie and Audrey took off in the private jet for a honeymoon on a remote island near Tahiti. After seeing them off in a shower of rice, Savannah and Blake went back upstairs to their room.

"You look a little tired," Blake observed, watching Savannah wander around the hotel room, absently picking up items and putting them down again.

She picked up the crystal paperweight from the desk and held it up to the light, tracing its facets with her fingertip. "It's been a whirlwind two days."

"You can say that again." She was tense. Too tense. Blake felt like he was walking on eggshells. "Does it bother you? Your father getting married again?"

"I'm used to it," she answered automatically. Then, irritated with herself, Savannah shook her head. "No. This time it's different. This time I think it just might last. Even if they haven't known each other very long."

"I didn't realize that there was a timetable for falling in love."

Why did she feel so let down? Her father was off on his honeymoon with a wonderful woman, she was alone in a hotel room in one of the most romantic cities in the world with a man who could make her knees weak just by looking at her, and here she was, feeling sorry for herself.

Because she wanted more, Savannah realized. She wanted to share more with Blake than just their work, or sex—as wonderful as that was. She'd shared her body with him. Now she wanted to share her heart.

The problem was, Savannah mused, she didn't think he would accept it.

"Of course, there isn't," she said. She nervously ran her palms down the front of her silk dress. "Don't pay any attention to me, Blake. I guess I'm just in a crazy mood." She tried a smile, which failed. "Probably PMS." She didn't tell him that although she hated to admit it, she'd just realized that deep down inside, she was a hopeless romantic. Just like her father.

Blake thought it was a great deal more than that, but decided not to argue. When would she trust him enough to stop these constant evasions?

"Did I tell you that you look beautiful?"

This time her smile was more genuine. "Yes. But I certainly wouldn't mind you saying it again."

"You're beautiful." He crossed the room to stand in front of her. "You'll always be beautiful to me."

There was something in his tone. Something new. Something serious. Something she didn't dare let herself think about.

"It's the dress," she managed through lips that had suddenly gone too dry for comfort. "You're so used to seeing me in jeans, you didn't realize how good I clean up." When she twirled like a young girl showing off a party dress, the handkerchief-hemmed skirt flared, displaying long, firm thighs.

"It's a lovely dress."

Actually, it was more than lovely. It reminded him of a spring garden. Created from some soft, floaty type of silk, the top of the dress hugged her curves like a lover's caress, the rounded neckline allowing a discreet but enticing glimpse of the tops of her breasts. The soft, watercolor-flowered print was reminiscent of the Monet Pamela's decorator had bought for the bedroom of their Bel Air mansion. He wondered if Savannah had been thinking of him when she'd bought the dress earlier that afternoon during her shopping trip with Audrey.

"But I don't think that's it."

"You don't?"

"No. But I suppose we should test this phenomenon further. Just to make sure I'm right. Why don't you take it off?"

Savannah smiled. "I thought you'd never ask." When she turned to go into the adjoining bathroom, Blake caught her wrist. "Here."

"All right. If that's what you want." When she would have turned off the light, he stopped her again.

"Leave it on. I want to look at you."

"But, Blake—"

"Leave it on." The request was softly couched, but it was a definite order, just the same. Savannah stared at him for a long time, wondering how she could have forgotten what a dangerous man he could be.

"I can't."

"Yes. You can. You have to, Savannah. If not for us, for yourself."

He made it sound so easy. Savannah was irritated by his smooth, self-assured tone. "You sound just like Justin," she ground out. "And the doctors. And Reggie."

"I'm waiting." He all but growled it.

"Please," she said, holding out her hand toward him. "We've been getting along so well. Don't do this, Blake. Don't ruin everything."

"I don't want to ruin anything, Savannah. But I'm sick and tired of supporting your warped image of yourself." His tone was clipped and hard, lacking in the warmth she'd come to expect.

"Now, are you going to take that dress off, or shall I take it off for you? Although, I have to warn you," he said, ignoring her startled, disbelieving gasp, "if you leave it up to me, sweetheart, you probably won't be able to wear it again."

Savannah looked up into his hard, implacable eyes and felt herself freezing inside. How could she have been so wrong about Blake? How could she not have seen that in his own way, he was even more ruthless than Jerry? And that she was just as helpless as she'd been eighteen months ago.

With fingers that had turned to ice, she began to lower the zipper, making a sound that was unnaturally loud in the hushed silence of the room. The silk caught in the zipper's metal teeth; Savannah yanked viciously at the material, causing it to rip.

"Blake . . ." She tried one more time.

Although it was the hardest thing he'd ever done, Blake held his ground. "I'm waiting."

"Damn you!" she whispered. She shrugged the dress off her shoulders, allowing it to slip to the floor in a puddle of floral silk.

She stood in front of him, trembling despite the warmth of the room, clad only in a satin lace-trimmed teddy, thigh-high ivory stockings and high heels. At the very time when any woman would want to appear her most attractive, Savannah was desperately aware of the ugly red scars marking her arms, her legs, her breast. She felt unbearably flawed; she felt miserably ugly.

His unwavering gaze shamed her straight through to her soul. Shame was a living, breathing thing twisting inside Savannah until she thought she'd suffocate from it. Tears streamed down her face.

"There." A rosy flush spread like a fever over the peaks of her breasts, up her throat, across her cheekbones. "Is that better?"

"It's a start."

Her flooding tears made his heart clench even as her bravado pulled at some hidden chord deep inside Blake—a warm, tender chord that was at direct odds with the cold fury aroused by the sight of her injuries.

The long jagged line on the inside of her arm was an even darker, crueler red than he'd imagined. As were the two scars twining around her thighs. The slash across her breast was a vicious purple. A sickening image of Savannah hurled through that window, shattering the glass into hundreds of razor-sharp pieces, pulsed through his head.

Blake's hand curled unconsciously into a fist. Although he'd never met Jerry Larsen, Blake knew he would receive enormous pleasure from killing the bastard for the torture he'd inflicted on Savannah.

The way he was looking at her had Savannah wishing for one of San Francisco's infamous earthquakes. If only the floor would open up and swallow her. Why wouldn't he say something?

Finally he did. "It's still a bit dark in here, don't you think?"

Just when she thought she was going to die of humiliation, her temper suddenly flared, numbing her conscious mind, blocking off the pain.

Her fury swept her around the room, and she turned on every lamp she could find until the room blazed with light. Finally Savannah stopped in front of him, her chin tilted, her eyes flashing, daring him to make the next move. Immersed in her exacerbation, she failed to notice that Blake's eyes had darkened.

"There. I took off the damn dress. All the lights are on. Dammit, are you happy now?"

He loved her like this. Almost naked, her eyes alive with passion, daring him. A jolt of desire stabbed through him; he went rigid with the effort to control it. The blazing fury in her gaze might have cooled the desire of most men, but Blake welcomed it. An angry woman was not an indifferent one.

"I think," he said slowly, "that any man would be happy if a gorgeous, sexy woman was standing in front of him wearing such a minuscule scrap of lace."

His calm statement threw her off. She'd bought the teddy on a whim while shopping with Audrey at Victoria's Secret. Although it had been ridiculously expensive, considering the scant amount of material involved in its creation, the gushing saleswoman had assured her that it would bring a man to his knees. Looking at Blake's expression, Savannah decided that she'd definitely gotten her money's worth.

"I want to hate you," she said, unable to forgive him so easily.

"I know."

"You hurt me."

"Don't you think I hurt myself, forcing you to do something so obviously painful?"

"Then, why...?"

"Because I wanted you to finally understand that I will always want you. Just the way you are." His fingers toyed with the strap of the teddy, pushing it off first one shoulder, then the other. "Especially the way you are right now. This is one incredibly sexy outfit."

Her self-consciousness, her embarrassment concerning her flawed body gradually faded. Her anger dissolved, and was replaced by a slow, soothing warmth.

"I bought it for you," she admitted in a whisper.

"Remind me to thank you," he said gruffly. "Later."

"Later," she agreed, her eyes held captive by his. She was still standing stiffly in front of him, but her skin, anticipating his wicked touch, had begun to tingle.

Blake surprised her. His hands went instead to her hair, where his clever fingers easily dispensed with the pins that had been holding it in an intricate figure eight at the nape of her neck. When the last of the pins joined the others on the plush carpet, her hair tumbled free.

"Much better," he murmured, appearing absorbed in its texture, the way the glowing lamplight brought out the deep blue tones in its jet color. He lifted one gleaming strand from her shoulders, wrapped it around his hand and buried his nose in it.

His lips pressed against her hair before moving to her temple, her earlobe, her neck. "You remind me of a Gypsy." His heated gaze settled on her face. "With your hair all wild black tangles around your face and your eyes as dark as midnight. You've no idea how many times I've dreamed of you looking this way. Looking at me this way."

His touch was achingly tender. Savannah basked in it. Bending his head, he kissed her bare shoulder. At the whisper-soft touch of his lips, Savannah swayed.

"I've dreamed of you, too," she admitted breathlessly, twining her fingers in his dark hair as she pressed her body more closely to his. "Wild, wicked, wonderful dreams."

It was all he'd been waiting to hear. With a muffled groan, he lowered his lips to her throat. Her scent was as potent as his passion, her taste was as warm as his blood. Picking her up in his arms, he carried her the few short steps to the bed.

Savannah clung to him. Her head was spinning with that familiar hunger that only he could create; her body was melting in his arms like molten gold. Breathless, wanting, needing, she murmured a small, inarticulate protest when he left her alone on the mattress long enough to take off his own clothes. And then he was back.

The peach satin smelled of her. Blake could have drowned in its heady scent. But since the temptation of her silky skin was even more irresistible, he dispensed with the material barrier.

She looked so fragile. And so beautiful. "I told you that first time—I don't care about any damn scars," he insisted in a husky voice that was not as steady as he would have liked. "They're nothing." He trailed his lips up her arm before moving to caress her breast. "Merely points of interest on a fascinating tour."

His teeth closed around the rosy tip of her breast, creating a flash of heat that spiraled to her very core. But even as Savannah gasped, he'd moved on, scattering kisses over her stomach, the inside of her thigh, the back of her knee. Her stomach, the inside of her other thigh, the back of her knee. His mouth was everywhere—tasting, tempting, racing on a crazed journey from her lips to her toes. And everywhere his lips touched, they left tormenting trails of ice and heat.

Savannah had thought she'd known what loving was. But even those other thrilling times with Blake had not prepared her for this. His mouth savaged her neck; his hands slid unerringly down her body, discovering secret, hidden flashpoints of pleasure. His intimate touch had her mind spinning, its heat had her skin drenched.

With a sense of greedy wonder, she responded, running her hands over Blake's body, delighting in the way his muscles rippled and clenched beneath her palms. She skimmed her lips over his flat stomach and felt him shudder. She flicked her tongue over his pebbly dark nipples and heard him groan.

Through her dazed senses, she realized that his impenetrable self-control was hanging by a razor's edge. The idea that she could cause such a primitive response made her giddy. The thought that she could make him weak and vulnerable—with a mere touch, or a kiss—filled her with a feminine thrill the likes of which she'd never known.

Wild, wanton, wicked cravings coursed through her. In a moment of abandon, she rose to her knees and ran her hands down his legs, her fingers exploring the corded muscles. Testing, she caressed with her lips the flesh her hands had warmed. And then with her teeth. Moaning her name between short, ragged breaths, Blake reached for her, but his touch was vague, almost dreamlike.

Blake Winters was the strongest, most powerful man she'd ever met. But somehow, he'd surrendered that power to her, and Savannah was delirious with the wonder of it.

The heat was like nothing he'd ever known. Her touch was like flame—his flesh burned with it. Her scent surrounded him in a sultry, hypnotic cloud. His body throbbed, his blood was swimming with a red-hot passion, frustration warred with pleasure, he wanted her to stop. He wanted her never to stop.

He was desperate to take her—now, before she succeeded in driving him insane—but his power was gone. It had flowed from him into her and for the first time in his life, Blake experienced true helplessness.

He was hers. Body. Mind. Soul. All hers. She felt it. She watched the need building in his eyes; she saw a primitive male passion burning there—a passion that was dangerously compelling. Unable to resist, she drove him closer to the precipice.

When she lay her heated body full length over his, Blake knew what true madness was. Sanity snapped. Everything savage—all the hazardous emotions civilization had taught him to keep locked away inside—burst free as if from an erupting volcano.

He'd never felt the need to possess a woman before, but now he found himself wanting all of Savannah Starr—not only her body, but her mind, her heart, her soul. All of her. As his entire world narrowed down to center on the feel of her moist, satiny flesh against his, Blake seized her shoulders and rolled her onto her back.

Their eyes locked. A promise, mutually felt, sizzled between them. In a moment of panic, Savannah tried to back away. But it was too late.

He plunged into her with a sudden, wild fury that surprised them both. Savannah's body arched, taut with the first uncontrollable climax. As she clung to him, frantic and strong, Blake was shaken by an unbidden, fierce desire for absolute possession. He dug his long fingers into her hips to keep her moving with him.

And then the power took them both.

"I TOLD YOU," Blake said, much, much later, "they don't matter."

They'd been lying together, arms and legs intertwined, basking in the afterglow of their lovemaking. Savannah's mind had been floating idly on gilt-edged clouds of ecstasy and she was in no hurry to come crashing back to reality.

"I don't want to talk about it."

"Tough." He took her chin in his and forced her rebellious gaze to his. "What do I have to do to convince you that your scars are hardly noticeable? Which is a moot point, because I'd still want you if you looked like the bride of Frankenstein."

"Thanks a heap," Savannah muttered. "I suppose I should be flattered by that charming comparison."

"Not necessarily. But don't you think it's time you grew up and started thinking for yourself?"

Angry color rose in her cheeks. "What are you talking about?"

"I'm talking about the fact that your mother—a stunningly beautiful but seriously disturbed woman—couldn't resist inflicting her daughter with her own poisonous fears."

His words hit too close to home for comfort. "You and Pop have been talking about me."

Blake didn't deny it. "He's worried about you."

"So he decided to hand me over to you for safekeeping?"

"I didn't say that."

"It was what you didn't say."

"Don't you think you're overreacting?" Blake asked.

Savannah folded her arms. "Perhaps." Her tone said otherwise.

"Savannah." He ran the back of his hand enticingly up the side of her face. "Sweetheart. As much as I can understand your feelings about your father's behavior, I really don't want to waste precious time arguing, when I could be making love to you."

That said, he gathered Savannah into his arms and began distracting her with long, deep kisses.

Blake feared that if he told her everything he and Reggie had discussed, he'd drive her away. And although he fully intended to be the last man in Savannah's life, he knew that after the debacle with Jerry Larsen, she was understandably apprehensive about possessive men.

As he felt Savannah succumbing to his skillful seduction, Blake decided that he'd simply have to take things slowly, until she realized that she belonged to him—as he belonged to her.

10

"I'VE GOT ANOTHER proposition for you," Blake said the next morning.

Savannah's smile was warm. "You know I can never resist one of your propositions."

She'd just stepped out of the shower. Her dark hair was piled in a casual twist on top of her head, she was clad solely in a fluffy white towel, and as his gaze settled on the beads of moisture glistening above her breasts, Blake almost forgot what he was going to say.

"How about, instead of going back to Mendocino right away, we stay in the city for a couple days?"

"But I still have to do the title song."

"It's only one song," Blake said.

"We don't have much time left."

"Enough that we can take some time off."

"But—"

"Sweetheart, it's called relaxing," he told her. "Being a workaholic myself, I can understand if you've never heard of the concept. But from what I've been told, the experience can actually be quite enjoyable. And if we were to go hog-wild and do it several days in a row, I believe that it's called a vacation."

He drew her into his arms, enjoying the fresh scent of soap lingering on her skin. "How about it, Savannah?" he coaxed seductively. "I can't think of anything I'd rather do than take a vacation with you."

It was so, so tempting. But impossible. Savannah put her hands on his arms and tried to draw away.

"But your film—"

"Why don't you let me worry about my film?" he suggested.

He was distracting her, sliding his fingertips tenderly, warmingly over her skin. Savannah wished he'd stop. She wished he'd never stop.

"I'd never forgive myself if I was responsible for the studio taking it away from you before it's finished."

"Never happen." He nuzzled her neck. "Because you'll come up with a dynamite song just in the nick of time. I have faith in you, Savannah."

Faith. That was a great deal like trust, wasn't it? Savannah tilted her head back and smiled up at him. "Last one back to bed is a rotten egg."

YEARS LATER, Savannah would look back on the following three days as a special, halcyon time apart. She and Blake played tourist, taking advantage of the myriad pleasures San Francisco had to offer.

They joined in the crazy commotion of Chinatown, stepping around the open stalls filled to overflowing with vegetables that crowded the sidewalks, and crates of fresh fish stacked along the curb. They drank in the sights of change: elderly Chinese men playing mahjongg and smoking fat cigars, while Chinatown's younger generation displayed an affinity for designer jeans and Sony Walkman radios.

Hand in hand, they strolled the streets of Cow Hollow, exploring the antique shops. In a boutique specializing in vintage clothing and accessories, Blake bought Savannah a Victorian pearl comb for her hair;

at a nearby shop filled to the rafters with nautical paraphernalia, she was thrilled to unearth a yellowed, ancient chart of the coastline where Blake's house had been built.

They stole kisses amid the pink bushes in Rhododendron Dell at Golden Gate Park, drank in the atmosphere of the City Lights bookstore, once the home of Beat writers Allen Ginsberg and Jack Kerouac, laughed as they fed each other chocolate at Ghirardelli Square and nearly froze when they joined a boatload of Japanese and German tourists on a harbor cruise to Alcatraz.

They ate crab salads at Fisherman's Wharf, watched the lights come on across the city from the Top of the Mark, listened to jazz in North Beach and danced the night away atop Nob Hill.

During this stolen time together, they talked, sharing childhood memories, adult experiences—all the things that had made them who they were, all the paths that had led to where they were today.

Working so closely together in Mendocino, sequestered from the outside world, both had gradually learned to trust each other. Now, that trust had led to intimacy—and, although neither Savannah nor Blake was prepared to be the one to first say the word out loud, to love.

Savannah experienced a joy she'd never known. Everything would have been perfect if only she could banish Jerry Larsen from her mind. Twice, she thought she saw him following them. The first time was in Chinatown, the second time on Fisherman's Wharf. But before she could be sure it was him, the man in question had drifted back into the crowd and disappeared.

And then there was that phone call. She'd picked up the ringing phone in their suite, only to hear a familiar, ominous silence on the other end. Slamming down the receiver, she'd been grateful that Blake was in the shower and hadn't seen her terrified response to what was undoubtedly a misdirected call.

Despite Jerry Larsen's presence hovering over Savannah like a threatening cloud, she managed, most of the time, to relax enough to bask in the warming comfort of Blake's love. Gradually, with each passing hour, came healing. Enough so that when Blake huskily suggested that they return to their hotel room in the middle of the day to make passionate love in the bright sunlight, she went into his arms willingly. Happily.

Although they weren't at all anxious to leave the city, on the morning of the fourth day, both reluctantly agreed that it was time—past time, really—to get back to work.

"Another couple of days and we should be done," Blake said as he maneuvered the car around the winding curves. It was raining again—a heavy, slanting rain that made the interior of the car seem more intimate than usual.

Savannah murmured a vague agreement. During these past days in San Francisco, as she'd basked in the pleasure of Blake's company, she hadn't allowed herself to think about work—about what would happen when she'd finished scoring the movie and returned to her own home in Malibu.

She'd miss him, she realized. Terribly. An unexpected melancholy settled over her, as cold and gray as the mists outside the car.

"You're awfully quiet," Blake said after they'd traveled several miles in silence. "Anything wrong?"

How could she tell him that she was missing him already? Hadn't he already assured her that he wasn't the kind of man to put strings on a relationship? Hadn't she been the one who insisted that she didn't want a commitment?

"Nothing." She forced a smile that wavered only slightly.

Even as she tried to reassure him, Savannah knew that Blake wasn't fooled for a minute. He saw too much. What if he realized that she loved him?

Love. The word came crashing down on her like a ten-ton weight. At first she had tried to deny it. She'd told herself that she was only responding to the romance of her father's wedding, of the blissful time she and Blake had shared.

But the more the word reverberated inside her head, the more Savannah knew that it was the truth. Somehow, when she wasn't looking, she had fallen hopelessly, inexorably in love with Blake Winters.

Now what?

Unable to answer, Savannah decided to follow Scarlett O'Hara's example and think about it tomorrow.

Blake would have given all the gross he expected to make on *Unholy Matrimony* in exchange for one quick look inside Savannah's head. Something had changed. The air was more charged. She'd become more tense. And distant.

He couldn't count the times he'd been on the brink of revealing his feelings. Over the past three days she'd shown a freedom of spirit, a joi de vivre, that he suspected she hadn't possessed since Jerry Larsen had hurt her. But now, as each mile brought them closer to the house, he could feel her pulling away, withdrawing inside herself. Frustrated, he gripped the steering wheel more tightly and glared out into the slanting silver mist.

They lapsed into an uncomfortable silence, neither one certain of the other's mood. Or of their own. The air grew nearly as chilly inside the car as out. Savannah cast a tentative glance at Blake.

His fingers had tightened around the steering wheel as if he was imagining them around someone's neck. His mouth and jaw were set in rigid, threatening lines. Right now it was impossible to believe that the person sitting beside her was the loving, laughing man who'd flown that colorful kite with her along San Francisco's rocky waterfront.

This man was the one she'd encountered that first stormy night. The man of the dark shadows and even darker moods. The man who'd reminded her so vividly of Dracula.

Noting Savannah's shiver, Blake reached out and turned up the car heater. But neither of them spoke the rest of the way up the mountain.

They finally arrived at Blake's house, only to find it shrouded in fog, looking as eerie as when Savannah had seen it for the first time.

"I'd forgotten how spooky this place can be," she murmured as they pulled up. It reminded her vaguely of the House of Usher. "I wouldn't be at all surprised to hear dogs howling."

Blake had thought, over these past days, that he'd been making headway. Obviously he'd been wrong. He arched a challenging black eyebrow, looking none too pleased by her quiet statement.

"Don't worry, the hounds of the Baskervilles are on temporary loan to Universal Studios." She would have had to be deaf to miss the acid sarcasm in his voice. "Does your reference to spooks and things that go bump in the night mean that I'm back to being Dracula?"

Savannah glanced over at him, deciding that it wouldn't be prudent to point out that at this moment, with the lambent anger smoldering in his fathomless eyes, there was a distinct resemblance.

"Only sometimes," she hedged.

"I suppose I should consider that progress," he decided gruffly.

The strange, uneasy mood followed them into the house. Blake started to carry the suitcases upstairs when something Savannah said garnered his instant attention.

"Oh, Blake, how sweet of you."

He turned, puzzled. "From Dracula to 'sweet' is one helluva quantum leap in two short minutes."

She was standing at the foot of the stairs, holding a long white box, tied with a red satin ribbon. It was a florist's box—the type used to send long-stemmed roses.

"This was on the foyer table. How on earth did you arrange to have them delivered so they'd be waiting when we got home?" She began to untie the elaborate bow.

Damn. Once again, he should have bought her flowers. Once again he hadn't. Then who? The answer, when it came, was chilling.

"Savannah—" Blake's harsh voice was almost a shout as he grabbed for the white box "—don't open—"

It was too late. Blake held his breath.

The box didn't hold flowers, after all, Savannah discovered. She stared down uncomprehendingly at the contents.

The Barbie doll was one of the few that weren't blondes. Indeed, her long black hair, beneath a frothy white lace wedding veil, was eerily similar to Savannah's. And if that weren't enough to frighten Savannah out of her wits, the doll's head had been cruelly twisted off its body.

"This is what happens to unfaithful women," the note pinned to the doll's wedding gown read.

Comprehension dawned. The doll, and the accompanying note, sent a frisson of icy fear up Savannah's spine. Her head began to swim. She reached out and clutched blindly at the banister.

Her knees turned to water. Just when she thought she was going to crumble to the floor, Blake shoved the bentwood foyer chair beneath her.

"Don't worry. It's going to be all right." He ran his hand down her hair in a clumsy attempt to soothe. Loath as he was to leave her, from the way all the color had fled Savannah's face, Blake realized that she was on the verge of fainting.

"Put your head between your knees," he advised. "I'll get some water."

He was back before Savannah had realized he'd gone. "Here." He put the glass in her hand, curling her numbed fingers around it.

Savannah drew in several deep breaths, willing the oxygen to clear her head. "I feel so foolish," she murmured, after taking a sip of the icy water. "I never faint."

She was huddled forward and although her hands, wrapped around the glass, were steady, they were white at the knuckles. She was still unnaturally pale and her eyes, wide with shock, appeared too large for the rest of her features.

Blake squatted beside the chair and held her stricken face in his hands. "I promise, Savannah. I'm not going to let that bastard near you."

Her head was spinning. But the resolve in Blake's tone fed Savannah's own courage. "I know."

They exchanged a long look fraught with emotion. Both had so many things to say. But this wasn't the time.

"He's crazy," she said in a papery voice that was close to a whisper.

"As a bedbug," Blake agreed grimly. "Why don't you call the police while I check the rest of the house and make sure he's gone."

"I'm coming with you."

"The hell you are."

"But—"

He cut her off with a fierce wave of his hand. "Have you forgotten that this is the guy who tried to kill you? The same guy the police can't find? Have you forgotten why you're staying here with me?"

Remarkably, she had. The events of the past few days had completely exorcised Jerry Larsen—and everything he represented—from her mind.

"You're staying right here and calling the cops," Blake said in a low, warning tone.

Anger flared, hot and quick. Savannah welcomed it; it took her mind off her fear. "You sound just like a character from *Police Beat*," Savannah said. "Didn't anyone ever warn you about taking your work to heart?"

"What's that supposed to mean?"

"I'm talking about the fact that you're happy to get an opportunity to act out all those adolescent male fantasies you wrote for your series."

"My what?" Frustration mixed dangerously with irritation in his eyes. "Are you saying that not wanting some lunatic to kill you is an adolescent male fantasy?"

Although Savannah realized that she may have stepped out of line with that one, she refused to flinch. "I really can take care of myself, Blake. I don't need a white knight or a hero to come dashing to my rescue."

It took a major effort, but Blake resisted pointing out that if she'd been so capable of avoiding Jerry Larsen's murderous rage the first time, she wouldn't have those damn scars she'd been so hung up about.

"The problem with your analysis, sweetheart, is that this is no fantasy." His fingers curved around her upper arms; his touch was firm, not gentle. "The maniac who decapitated that doll isn't the product of some screenwriter's warped imagination. He's real. And he's after you."

His grip tightened as the idea of Jerry Larsen getting this close to Savannah sent ice coursing through Blake's veins. "And you can call me a chauvinist or any other unflattering thing you want if it makes you feel better, but the truth is that I care about you, dammit."

His intense expression made her stomach flutter. "You certainly don't sound very thrilled about it."

"It was not having a choice that I wasn't wild about."

Savannah could certainly identify with that. "I care about you, too," she said softly.

"Then stay here. So I don't have to worry about you."

Savannah heard the steel in his voice and decided that discretion was in order. "All right."

Her sudden turnabout earned a sharp, suspicious look. "So we're agreed? You'll call the cops while I search the house?"

Savannah dipped her dark head. "You're right. It's probably the best plan."

Blake didn't believe a word of her sweetly issued acquiescence, but each second he stood here arguing gave Larsen, if he was in the house, further opportunity to escape. He went into the parlor, returning with a pistol.

"Here," he said, handing it to Savannah. "Just in case."

She looked at the gun as if it were a cobra, poised to strike. Then, gingerly, she took it from Blake's outstretched hand. "I don't like guns."

"If Larsen suddenly pops up, I have a feeling you might like this one a lot better," Blake said dryly. "Besides, you don't have to worry about actually shooting the guy because it's only a starter's pistol. Justin left it here after officiating at some celebrity north-coast ten-kilometer charity run. How good are you at bluffing?"

"Very good. After all, I am—was—an actress." She gave him a reassuring smile. "Go check the house, Blake. I'll be fine. I promise."

His eyes, warm with emotion, swept over her face. "You're a lot more than fine, Savannah Starr," he murmured. Bending his head, he gave her a quick, hard kiss that made her head start spinning all over again. And then he was gone.

Savannah called the Los Angeles police and talked with Detective Robert Peterson, who proved every bit as distant as he'd been the first time she'd talked with him. Although he promised that he'd contact the county sheriff's office and have them send someone out to the house, his tone was brusque and officious, lacking any personal warmth.

Remembering the unwavering support she'd received from the detective who'd first handled her face, Savannah found herself wishing that Mike McAllister had chosen any other time to take his vacation.

After she made the call, Savannah picked up the starter pistol and followed Blake upstairs.

She found him, standing in front of the open door to the guest room. "Dammit," he growled, "I thought you promised to stay put."

"I had my fingers crossed." Savannah stared in at the destruction Jerry had wrought.

All her clothes had been scattered around the room. Obscenities had been scrawled on the dressing-table mirror in lipstick. Savannah picked up a high-necked, long-sleeved nightgown from the floor. Blake thought it looked like something from the wardrobe department of *Little House on the Prairie*. He realized that the nightgown, along with the rest of her clothes, including those ugly white cotton bras, had been vandalized to give Jerry Larsen some sick kind of sexual pleasure.

The idea caused gall to rise in his throat. The guy was lucky he'd gotten out of the house before they returned home. Because if he'd gotten his hands on him, Blake decided, he would have killed him.

"Why?" she whispered. Her fingers traced the long rents made in the snow-white cotton fabric by an unseen knife.

"It doesn't matter." He plucked the nightgown from her icy hands and tossed it onto the bed. "Because you weren't going to wear this stuff again, anyway."

Savannah thought about the suitcase filled with all the lacy lingerie that she'd purchased in the city. And how favorably Blake had responded to those silk-and-satin confections. "That still doesn't give him any right to do this."

Blake, watching the anger rise in Savannah's cheeks, reflected that she was the bravest woman he'd ever met. Any other woman of his acquaintance—hell, most people—would be screaming their heads off about now. Or lying on the floor in a dead faint. Savannah, on the other hand, was furious.

"We're going back to San Francisco."

"But Detective Peterson is sending over the sheriff," Savannah said.

"Okay, we'll stay here long enough to give him our statement. Then, as soon as we get the formalities over with, I'm taking you back to the city."

"Why?"

"I've got a friend on the San Francisco police force. That guy I told you about. The one who was a consultant on *Police Beat*. He'll find you a safe place to hide until Larsen is apprehended."

"But your film," Savannah argued. "If we don't get back to work on *Unholy Marriage*, you'll be over deadline."

"The hell with the damn deadline."

The idea that he'd jeopardize his beloved film for her proved, more than anything else, that Blake didn't consider what was happening between them to be a casual affair any more than she did. Savannah, moved more than she could have imagined by his gritty statement, was on the verge of confessing her own feelings when the deep sound of a gong reverberated through the house.

"That's the front door," Blake said. "It's probably the sheriff."

"I suppose so."

They were standing there, in the middle of the trashed bedroom, staring into each other's eyes. Neither moved. It was as if their feet had been nailed to the floor.

The gong sounded again. "I'd better go answer it." Blake appeared no more eager to budge than Savannah was anxious to have him leave.

"Yes." The moment had passed. Savannah didn't, couldn't, decide whether she was feeling regret or relief. She held out her hand, enjoying the reassuring warmth of Blake's fingers as they curled around hers. "And I'm not leaving," she said as they went down the stairs together.

THE MENDOCINO SHERIFF was polite and efficient. Acting as if such vandalism was an everyday occurrence, he took their statements, promised to stay in touch with the Los Angeles police, and assured them that he'd have his men comb the woods around the house.

"Don't worry, Ms. Starr," he promised. "The guy's not going to hurt you." He put on his slicker, shook hands with Blake and Savannah, then turned to leave. "Oh, there is just one little thing."

"Yes?" Savannah said.

"If you wouldn't mind." A dark flush rose from above his collar. "My wife's a real big fan of yours. Do you think, I mean, if you wouldn't mind . . ."

Savannah recognized the syndrome. No longer the efficient professional, the sheriff had turned into a tongue-tied fan. "Of course. Do you have a piece of paper and a pen?"

He whipped them out. "Her name's Melanie."

"Melanie," Savannah murmured as she signed the autograph.

"She was named after your mama," the sheriff blurted out. "Melanie Raine sure was a beautiful woman," he said admiringly.

"She certainly was," Savannah agreed. Tragically beautiful, as it had turned out.

"Yes, ma'am, the lady was prettier than a speckled pup."

Despite the grave reason for his visit, Savannah smiled. She handed him the paper. "Here you are."

He glanced down at the autograph, his expression that of a man who'd just been given the key to Fort Knox. "Thanks a lot, Ms. Starr," he said. "My wife's gonna love this!"

Tipping his hat, he opened the door and disappeared into the slanting rain.

"Pretty as a speckled pup," Blake mused, once they were alone again. "I'll have to remember that one—next time I'm trying to seduce a beautiful woman into my bed."

Savannah smiled. Blake slowly lowered his head. His lips were almost to hers when the phone rang. Frustrated, he picked up the receiver.

"Hello? Oh, yeah, we've been waiting to hear from you. Sure, she's right here." He held the phone out to Savannah. "It's a Detective McAllister."

"Hello, Mike," Savannah greeted the detective warmly. "You've no idea how happy I am that you're back. How was your vacation?"

There was a moment's pause on the other end of the line. "Great," the detective said. "We had a terrific time. But I didn't call to talk about my vacation."

He'd always worried about her too much, Savannah considered. In fact, there had been times if she hadn't known that he was madly in love with his wife, she would have suspected the detective of having a slight crush on her.

"I suppose Detective Peterson has filled you in on what's been happening."

"Yeah. And that's what I'm really calling about," he said. "We got him, Savannah."

Relief rushed over her in cooling waves. "Really? That's wonderful news!" She looked over at Blake and smiled. "They caught Jerry."

"He was picked up about an hour ago breaking into your Malibu house. We'll need you to testify about the other stunts Larsen's been pulling—the calls, the roses, that doll, and tearing apart your room at Winters's place—but don't worry, Savannah, we've got enough on the guy to make sure that he'll never bother you again."

"Thank you so much, Mike," she said, her voice filled with relief. "I owe you one."

"Hey." He sounded embarrassed. "It's my job."

After hanging up, Savannah turned to Blake. "You know that new line you wanted to try out?" she asked silkily. Her heart went into her smile as she wrapped her arms around his waist. "The one about the speckled pup?"

Blake smiled down at her. "It seems to ring a bell."

"Why don't we go upstairs," she suggested in a voice that was half honey, half smoke. "And see if it works."

"I thought you'd never ask." He slowly lowered his head. For the second time in as many minutes, his lips were almost touching hers when the phone rang again.

"Damn. I think I like it a lot better when the power's out," he muttered, releasing Savannah to snatch up the receiver. "This had better be good," he growled. "Oh, hi, Justin. No, nothing's wrong. You just caught me at a bad time." He looked over at Savannah and waggled his dark eyebrows in a lusty fashion that earned a dazzling smile in return. "What's up?"

"The Los Angeles police contacted me today about Jerry Larsen," Justin said. "Why didn't either of you say anything about the man's threats while we were in San Francisco?"

"Savannah didn't want to put a pall over her father's wedding," Blake explained.

"Well, after the detectives left, I started worrying about her."

"You can stop worrying. She's safe. The L.A. cops just picked up the guy," Justin assured him.

"That's good news." Blake heard the older man's relieved sigh over the telephone wires. "So now we just have one other little problem."

"If you're talking about the deadline—"

"No. Not that. It's me. I'm stuck."

"Stuck?"

"Now that I know you're both safe, I realize that I overreacted, but after talking with those detectives, I couldn't stop worrying. I tried to call the house—several times, as a matter of fact—but there was no answer."

"Savannah and I decided to stay in the city for a few days," Blake said. "We just got home. I guess I forgot to turn on the answering machine when we left."

"That's undoubtedly the case," Justin agreed. "Well, anyway, I was on the way to Mendocino, to make certain you and Savannah were all right, when the Jag broke down. I'm calling from my car phone a few miles down the road from your house. Do you think you could come and get me?"

Blake turned toward Savannah. "He's broken down a few miles down the mountain."

"Well," Savannah said with a wry smile, "you've been absolutely dying for an opportunity to play Superman and rescue someone. Here's your chance." She remembered how frightening that dark road had appeared in the rainstorm.

After assuring Justin that he was on his way, Blake gathered Savannah once again into his arms.

"Justin and I have been friends for a long time. And as much as I appreciate his apparent matchmaking efforts in getting us together, his timing definitely leaves a lot to be desired."

"You can say that again." Her sigh echoed her own disappointment.

He tipped her face up with a finger and kissed her. "I'll be back before you know it." A wicked glint came into his eyes—one she was beginning to recognize. "In the meantime, why don't you go upstairs and change into one of those frilly things you bought in the city?"

"But Justin will be coming back with you, and—"

He kissed her again, cutting off her protest. "No problem. I'll simply tell him that you're still upset over the shock of Larsen breaking into the house and have gone to bed."

"Good idea." Savannah couldn't suppress her saucy grin. "And it's almost the truth," she said, breathless at the expectation of making love to Blake again. This time, Savannah decided, she'd surprise him. This time, she'd seduce him.

Blake could see emotion shimmering in her dark eyes. Her curved lips were full and filled with sensual promise and the soft hue of late summer roses bloomed in her cheeks.

Gazing down into her face, Blake decided that if the early Puritan settlers of Salem had witnessed Savannah Starr looking like this, they would have burned her at the stake.

Mine, he thought with a certain mind-stunning wonder. *The woman is mine.*

Dragging her to him, Blake gave her one long, hard kiss that left her head spinning. "Keep that thought."

Then, with one last look, he disappeared out the door, into the night.

11

Savannah was humming as she ran the water into the deep, lion-paw-footed copper bathtub.

"I love him."

She tossed some bath salts under the tap and watched them turn the bathwater to a deep green foam.

"I love him."

For good measure, she tossed in another handful.

"And when he gets back, I'm going to show him exactly how much."

Smiling with anticipation, she went downstairs, retrieved her suitcase and carried it up to Blake's bedroom. A new storm had blown in from the Pacific. Rain streamed down the windows, lightning flashed across the dark sky. Immersed in the warmth of her recently discovered love, Savannah wasn't at all bothered by the coastal storm.

"Boy, am I going to show him."

Riffling through her new cache of silk and satin, she retrieved one particular item she hadn't had the nerve to wear. Until now.

The strapless, lace gown was as black as the devil, as sheer as a whisper and as tempting as sin. After laying the gown on the bed, to be put on after her bath, Savannah peeled off her jeans and sweater. Crossing the room, she retrieved Blake's black robe from the closet, shrugged into it and went back into the bathroom.

While she waited for the deep tub to fill, she lit the numerous white candles that Blake had put in every room, in response to the frequent power outages caused by coastal storms.

The ancient, but ever-reliable boiler was doing its job. The hot water rose in the copper tub, sending steam billowing upward in a fragrant cloud. The mysterious, Oriental perfume of the bath salts mingled seductively with the vanilla scent of the candles.

Savannah had just turned off the water when the lights in Blake's adjoining bedroom went out. Her pulse jumped.

"It's the storm," she said firmly, as if saying the words aloud would make them true. "The lights go out all the time. They were out the night I first came here."

The candle flames made shadows dance and jump on the bathroom wall like St. Elmo's fire; outside, the wind moaned like a lost spirit. Then Savannah heard a board squeak.

"Blake?" How strange that he'd be back so soon, Savannah considered, her nerves beginning to hum. He must have forgotten something.

When there was no answer, panic lodged in her throat, making it hard to breathe. She licked her suddenly dry lips and tried again. "Blake?" The flat sound of her voice scared her.

"This is an old house," Savannah reminded herself in a trembling whisper. "Old houses always make noises at night." There was another ominous squeak that made her skin turn to gooseflesh. "Creaks and groans come with the territory," she insisted as she tugged the sash on Blake's robe tighter. "It doesn't mean anything."

The sound came again. When she looked out into the hallway only to discover that all the lights had gone out, creating a well of darkness as deep and black as a tomb, Savannah felt a flicker of absolute terror.

She was a woman alone in this huge, dark Gothic house. All the movies about women in peril she'd ever seen flashed through her mind, causing fear to billow like smoke from a wildfire.

Her terrified mind was whirling, her thoughts disconnected. Flickering through them were images of the decapitated Barbie doll, her torn underwear, of Jerry. In a strange, surrealistic, out-of-body flashback, she saw herself flying through the window, viewed the ambulance speeding through the night, watched as the doctors sewed up her jagged wounds, saw the crimson blood—her blood—everywhere.

"Don't be ridiculous," she insisted in a voice that was shakier than she would have liked. She was desperately trying to hold back the growing fear that was eating at her flimsy barrier of control. "Jerry's been caught. Detective McAllister said so."

Another sound. This time, the unmistakable step of a foot on a stair. Her muscles tensed; panic buzzed in her head. It was only the cat, Savannah struggled to convince herself. Come for his dinner.

Frantic, she looked around for Blake's starter pistol, only to remember that she'd left it down the hall, in her vandalized bedroom. Calling herself a fool for getting so paranoid about the simple sound of a house settling, she grabbed Blake's Oscar from its bedroom shelf.

Perhaps, the thought suddenly occurred to her, she was dreaming. Perhaps this was merely a new version of the nightmare that hadn't haunted her since she'd fallen in love with Blake.

But as much as she would have welcomed the return of that horrific dream right now, the reality of the Oscar was undeniable. The statuette was real and heavy and tangible under her frozen fingers, forcing her to accept the nightmarish fear that had made her grasp it was all too real.

Holding the Oscar in front of her, she quietly slipped out the bedroom door and began to creep, barefoot, down the narrow hallway, into the swallowing darkness.

She was almost home free. Savannah had just begun to breathe again when Jerry Larsen appeared at the top of the stairs.

"Hello, Savannah."

Lightning flashed outside a nearby window, revealing his handsome, unthreatening face. His tone was calm, as if there were nothing unusual about breaking into another man's home.

Hysteria surged up; Savannah pushed it down. "What are you doing here, Jerry?"

"I'd say that should be obvious." He glanced past her, down the hall to her bedroom. "Didn't you get any messages?"

Savannah rubbed her temple, where her pulse was beginning to pound. "I got them."

"Then you'll understand why I came. Why I have to punish you."

Somehow, she would deal with this. "How did you get away from the police?" she asked, forcing herself to remain calm.

He laughed at that, but the cruel sound held no humor. "I didn't get away. They never found me in the first place."

Comprehension dawned, cold and harsh. Savannah felt beads of icy moisture form on her forehead. "You made those calls yourself," she said. "You pretended to be Mike McAllister. And then you called pretending to be Justin, to get Blake out of the house."

"Maybe now you'll appreciate my talent." Venom poisoned his voice, reminding Savannah of the night he'd tried to kill her. But he continued to smile, while Savannah knew the blood had drained from her face.

"But I always appreciated your talent," she protested frantically. "Didn't I ask Justin to get you that HBO special?"

"You could have done more."

"Just tell me," she said. "Tell me what you want, and I'll do it." She stepped toward him, stopping when she heard the quick, deadly click of a pistol.

"It's too late for that, Savannah." The gun was steady, but a wild hatred raged in his light blue eyes. "In the beginning, I thought you were a good girl. That you weren't like other women. I thought you loved me, and I believed you when you promised to help my career."

"But I did."

"Not enough. You made me a laughingstock of the tabloids."

"Nobody believes anything they read in those things," Savannah protested, wishing that it were true.

"Shut up!" He cut her off by waving the gun in her face. "You ruined my career. You testified in court that I was some sort of crazy, possessive monster. That your accident was my fault."

She'd seen that frantic, deadly light in his eyes before—right before she'd gone flying through the window. Biting her lip, Savannah didn't respond.

"But we both know that you deserved what happened to you, Savannah. You ruined my career, then you slept with another man, just like you've been sleeping with Winters."

This time, Savannah didn't bother to argue that she'd never slept with that other actor. Experience had taught her that Jerry wouldn't believe her, anyway. As for her relationship with Blake, how could this horrid man even begin to understand love?

"I thought about killing Winters, too," Jerry mused. "But then I decided that it'd be better if I left him alive. So he can be the one to find your body. So he'll be the one to go to prison for your murder."

"No one would believe that Blake would kill me."

"Wouldn't they?" His eyes reminded her of a snake's: cold, flat and deadly. "The man's already been accused of trying to kill one unfaithful woman," he reminded her. "When you're found dead in his bedroom, the evidence will speak for itself."

His planned scenario was insane. As was he. Unwilling to be his victim ever again, she suddenly sprang forward, hurling the Oscar at him, pushing him aside. Her strength momentarily threw him off balance and as she raced down the stairway, Savannah heard him curse. She didn't stop to look around.

She managed to reach the front door, only to discover that he'd double-bolted it. Before her numbed fingers could unfasten the bolt, Jerry was on top of her. Grabbing her streaming hair, he dragged her to an abrupt halt.

"Dammit," he said through gritted teeth, "we've acted out this scene before." His hand tightened on her hair; his furious red face was just inches from hers. "This time you're not going to get away. This time you're going to find out what happens to unfaithful women."

His hand went to her throat, his fingers applying enough pressure for her to feel the fury behind them. Stalling for time, knowing that Blake would soon discover that Justin's car wasn't broken down and return home, Savannah decided to try again.

"Jerry, please. What happened last time was an accident. I know you. I know that you'd never purposely hurt me."

"Oh, no?" His dangerous grin turned Savannah's blood to ice. "You didn't know my mother, did you?" he asked. "Of course, you didn't—" he answered his own rhetorical question "—because she was already dead when you and I met."

Savannah remembered him telling her about the tragic accident that had taken his mother's life. She'd fallen asleep while smoking, Jerry had said. At the time, he'd seemed honestly heartbroken. "She died in a fire."

"A fitting punishment," he said, "for leaving her husband and seven-year-old son behind in Seattle and running off to California with that sailor." His mouth twisted; hatred blazed in his eyes.

Savannah stared at him in horror; new fear clutched at her throat.

"I paid her a visit after I came to L.A. to work in the comedy clubs. She pretended that she was glad to see me," Jerry continued. "But I knew that she was only waiting for me to leave and him to come home—so she could go to bed with him, like the adulterous slut she was. So when she turned her back, I picked up the ashtray—it was a big ceramic one from Yosemite—and hit her over the head."

Jerry ignored Savannah's startled gasp. He was staring off into the distance, as if watching the murderous scene. "I dragged her into the bedroom, laid her on the bed, lit a cigarette and put it between her fingers. Then I used her lighter to set fire to the bedspread and drapes, and left."

His fingers tightened around her throat, causing pain. "The police called with the tragic news later that night."

The fury in his eyes had disappeared; in its place was a calm composure that frightened Savannah far more than his earlier anger.

She risked a glance at the grandfather clock. Blake had been gone for more than thirty minutes; by now he should have realized that he'd been sent on a wild-goose chase. Keep talking, she told herself.

"I'm not your mother, Jerry," she said softly, trying to hold back the fear that was tearing down her control.

"No." He looked at her, and his eyes narrowed as his gaze swept over her face. "You're not. But you're just like her." There was a line of sweat above his lip that he did not bother to wipe away. "And now you'll have to be punished, too."

"Jerry." She placed a hand on his arm. "Perhaps I did make a mistake," she said in a gentle voice that trembled only slightly. "Perhaps I did underestimate your talent. Maybe I didn't appreciate you enough. But I was never unfaithful."

"You were."

"No." She licked her lips, swallowing the metallic taste of terror. "I wasn't. That night you were waiting at my house—the night I came home from the wrap party with that actor—we were only friends, Jerry. Less than friends. We'd worked on the picture together. He meant nothing to me. Less than nothing."

Her eyes were soft and guileless; her fingers stroked his sleeve. "How could he? How could any man compare to you?"

Seeds of doubt appeared in Jerry's eyes. The hand that had been around her neck caught hold of her chin and held her innocent gaze to his intent one. "You didn't sleep with him?"

"No," she said truthfully.

"And Winters? What about him?"

"I don't even like him." It took every ounce of Savannah's acting ability to tell that lie. "Since I couldn't act any longer, Justin talked me into working with the man, Jerry. I'm scoring his picture. That's all."

Her fingers gingerly crept up his sleeve to his shoulder. When he didn't jerk away, she placed her palm against his cheek, feeling the muscle tense beneath her fingertips. "To tell you the truth, I can't wait to finish and get away from this horrid old place."

"I don't know why," Jerry said slowly. Savannah could tell that he wanted to believe her. "Winters is famous."

"So are you," she insisted. "Everyone who saw your HBO special said that you were brilliant. Even Blake remarked on your talent."

"Blake Winters said I was talented?" His grip on her loosened fractionally.

"Yes, he did. Honestly."

His eyes went blank for a minute, then cleared. "Maybe, since you're working with him, you could talk him into giving me a part in his next picture."

Savannah felt exactly like Alice after she'd fallen down the rabbit hole and ended up at the Mad Hatter's tea party. One minute Jerry was confessing to the murder of his mother and threatening to kill her; the next minute he was asking her to get him a part in Blake's next picture.

"I could ask," she agreed breathlessly. "I'm sure he'd be wild about the idea."

"A Blake Winters picture," Jerry murmured. "Starring Jerry Larsen." The hand that was holding the pistol lowered as his other hand stroked her cheek. "It does have a certain ring to it."

"A wonderful ring," Savannah agreed. She turned her head ever so slightly, so that her lips brushed against his fingers. "I'd be so proud of you, Jerry."

"You're damn right you would be," he agreed. "Because I'd be a star." His fingers traced the scar that ran from her ear to the corner of her lips. "Especially since, let's face it, sweetheart, with your face messed up like it is, your acting days are over. You are, as they say in the trades, a has-been."

Amazingly, these past days with Blake had made Savannah forget completely the physical scars this man had inflicted on her.

"You're lucky I still find you sexy," he said as he untied the sash of the robe. "Because with those scars, you'd have a hard time getting any other man."

She recognized the look that moved across his face as he opened the robe and viewed the seashell-pink teddy she was wearing underneath. Murder had been momentarily forgotten in favor of lust.

"Nice," he murmured. He pushed the robe off her shoulders, onto the floor. "Very nice."

His mouth approached hers. Savannah curled her left hand into a fist by her side and braced herself for his kiss just as the grandfather clock began to strike the hour. To keep her sanity, Savannah counted each gong: one, two, three . . .

When the clock finally chimed ten, Jerry, intent on deepening the kiss, thrust his tongue between her lips. Savannah bit down. Hard. Surprised, he jerked his head back just as she hit him as hard as she could, right in the center of his face.

Furious, he pulled away with a bloodcurdling scream. The gun fell to the hardwood floor. Jerry began scrubbing at his mouth with the back of his hand, and when he viewed the bright red blood, mingling with the blood pouring from his nostrils, murder rose in his eyes once again.

But Savannah didn't see it. She was running through the labyrinth of hallways and down the stairs, to the basement.

It was dark. And damp. As she groped her way down the steep stairs and along the wall, Savannah hoped that she could elude Jerry long enough for Blake to return.

"Savannah?"

He'd followed her. Trembling, Savannah tried to hide in the shadows.

"You'll never get away, Savannah. By the time your lover realizes that it was me who called him, you'll be dead."

Trapped. The word reverberated hollowly in her mind. Numb with fear, Savannah crouched behind a large trunk next to the boiler when something suddenly brushed against her legs. Covering her mouth with her hand to stop her scream, she looked down at the cat, who had begun mewing for his dinner. She tried petting him, which only made him mew louder. Frustrated, she pushed him away, hoping that he'd take the hint and leave, but instead he let out an irritated yelp and refused to go.

The sound captured Jerry's immediate attention. "You can't hide from me, Savannah," he called out. "Not after I've spent all those lonely months in prison thinking of all the ways to get even with you."

Savannah was shaking, but she refused to answer. Although she couldn't see him in the blackness, she could hear Jerry approaching. She wanted to run. To scream. When she heard the deadly, unmistakable click of the gun's safety again, she knew that she had run out of time.

She saw Jerry's shadow getting closer. Just when Savannah thought that perhaps she really was going to die, the room was suddenly flooded with a blinding light.

Jerry spun around. Savannah followed his gaze to the foot of the stairs, where Blake was standing.

"What the hell do you think you're doing, Larsen?" he asked, far too quietly.

If Jerry was terrified by the larger man's sudden appearance, he didn't reveal it. "I'm getting even."

"For what?"

Jerry looked taken aback by Blake's calm question. His nose was still bleeding; he wiped the blood away with his sleeve. It took him a long time to answer. "For everything."

Blake moved closer. "I see. So, since you didn't manage to kill Savannah the first time, you've come back to finish the job?"

"That's right." Jerry appeared relieved that Blake seemed to understand. "She deserves to die, Winters. You, of all people, should understand that."

Blake continued to approach. "Why me, of all people?"

Savannah, who'd prudently remained silent, knew that Blake was at his most dangerous when he used that quiet, logical tone.

"Because of your wife," Jerry explained, sniffling. He pressed his hand to his nose to stop the steady trickle of blood, then flinched from the pain. "She screwed around, so you had to kill her."

"You shouldn't believe everything you read, Larsen." He was now only a few feet away. "I didn't try to kill Pamela."

Jerry laughed. "Sure, you gotta *say* that," he agreed. "That's the same thing I told my lawyer and the cops. And those prison shrinks. But we both know the two-timing bitches got what they deserved."

The seemingly casual conversation was making Savannah increasingly nervous. Although it was two against one, the gun Jerry was holding in his hand definitely tilted the odds in his favor.

Cold sweat ran down Blake's back. It hadn't taken him long to realize that he'd been played for a damn fool. Cursing himself for falling for Larsen's act, he'd raced back to the house as fast as he could. When he'd found it ominously dark, he'd felt his heart lurch. Then he'd viewed the dark stain on the foyer floor and tasted blood in his own mouth.

Desperate, Savannah looked around the room for a weapon. Any weapon. When her searching eyes met Blake's guarded ones, she saw him glance fleetingly at the boiler beside her before returning his impenetrable gaze to Jerry Larsen's face.

The boiler. Of course! Why hadn't she thought of it? While Blake kept Jerry talking about the untrustworthiness of women, Savannah inched over and flipped the pressure release valve. A loud, hot gust of steam instantly captured Jerry's attention.

Blake swung. Shaken by the sudden blow, Jerry slid bonelessly down the wall. Blake's fists pounded savagely into his already bloody face.

"Blake! I'm all right."

Savannah was momentarily stunned by Blake's explosive response. Blake's temper, once unleashed, was a frightening thing to behold. Her feelings for him—her love—had blinded her, making her forget that he was a man of strong emotions—emotions that she'd once found frighteningly dangerous.

Blake was straddling Jerry, his knee painfully into the other man's chest, his long fingers wrapped around his throat.

"You're going to kill him," Savannah said, pulling ineffectually at Blake's rigid arm. "Please, Blake, he isn't worth it. He didn't hurt me. I'm all right."

Jerry's face had turned a dangerous shade of purple; his eyes were bulging and blood streamed from his fractured nose and split lip. The cellar reeked with the smell of his fear.

Blake looked up at Savannah, then down in mute surprise at his victim. He was actually on the verge of killing a man. And although he'd admittedly seen more than his share of violence during his early years in the Texas oil patch, Blake would never have thought himself capable of murder.

Until now. Until Savannah. The power of love was terrifying.

"The bastard tried to kill you," he argued. "Twice." A core of violence lingered in his eyes. But his fingers loosened their grip.

Savannah sank to her knees beside him. "But he didn't. Because you saved me."

Blake frowned as he lifted a finger to the darkening bruises on Savannah's neck. "I should kill him just for this."

"He isn't worth it," she repeated softly.

"No. He isn't." Blake took a deep, head-clearing breath and stood, yanking the cowering, sobbing man to his feet. "Come on, Larsen, you've got a date with the police."

THE SHERIFF ARRIVED within minutes, his expression and his demeanor far more grim and professional than it had been earlier, when he'd asked Savannah for her autograph.

After Jerry Larsen had been taken off to jail, Blake pulled a still-unsteady Savannah into his arms. She'd put his robe on again and although she was dwarfed by the heavy folds of black terry cloth, he realized that she wasn't as fragile as he'd thought that first night.

"You're shaking," he murmured against her hair.

She clung to him—clung tightly. "So are you."

Blake didn't argue. He'd thought, during the seemingly endless interview with the sheriff, that he'd overcome his rage. His fear. But now, holding Savannah in his arms, it all came crashing back down on him.

"When I saw that blood..." An enormous lump rose in his throat. Blake brought his mouth down on hers, hard. He needed the sweet, familiar taste of her to convince himself that she really was safe.

"I thought you were..." Blake couldn't make himself say the word. "I thought I was too late," he managed instead, in a voice roughened with emotion. "I thought I'd lost you."

Love swept through Savannah—overwhelmingly. She tilted her head back and gave him a wobbly smile. "I'm not that easy to get rid of." Her eyes filled with the tears she'd held back for too long.

Blake kept his touch gentle as he brushed the glistening moisture from her cheeks with his bruised and swelling knuckles. "I need you, Savannah. And that scares the hell out of me."

"I know." Her hands trembled from emotions too complex to catalog as she lifted them to his face. "Would it make you feel any better if I told you that I need you, too? And that it scares the hell out of me?"

"There's more."

Savannah waited.

"I love you."

"I know that, too." It almost frightened her—the sheer wonder of it. "And you've no idea how glad I am to hear you finally say it. Since I've been in love with you forever."

Feeling better, he lifted an eyebrow. "Forever?"

"Well, it seems like forever."

His arms tightened around her and he lowered his forehead to hers. "I know the feeling," he murmured. "Very well." They stood there for a long, luxurious time, drawing strength and comfort from each other.

The storm continued to rage. Outside, the wind wailed and lightning arced across the night sky. Caught up in the magic of the moment, neither Savannah nor Blake noticed.

"Savannah?"

"Mmm?"

Damn. It was not at all the way he'd planned it. He had intended to put a bottle of very good champagne on ice. There should be music and flowers. He'd even spent the major part of the drive north from San Francisco mentally penning a pretty proposal. But the clever, persuasive words had fled his mind.

Blake remembered how Savannah had accused him of being a creature of the dark. During those first few days she'd spent at his house, he'd reluctantly come to accept the fact that her unflattering description was more accurate than she could have realized.

At least, it had been, until she'd managed to infiltrate his life like a dazzling ray of bright summer sunshine, banishing the darkness forever.

Abandoning words for action, Blake tucked his arm firmly behind Savannah's knees, scooped her up and began carrying her up the curving stairs.

"Blake, what are you doing?"

"What does it look like?" He shifted her in his arms. "I'm taking you upstairs to my bed. And then, when I have you exactly where I want you, I'm going to persuade you to marry me."

Surprise, pleasure, love—all rushed into her eyes. "You sound awfully sure of yourself," she murmured as he marched purposefully down the hallway.

"You've got it all wrong, sweetheart," he said as he entered the bedroom.

From the sight of the incredibly sexy nightgown spread out on his bed like an ebony lace invitation, Blake realized that Savannah had been planning an identical scenario for tonight. Encouraged, he laid her tenderly, almost reverently, on the mattress.

"I'm not that sure of myself at all," he admitted as he began undressing her with hands that weren't nearly as steady as he would have liked. "But I am sure of you."

In the stuttering white light of the storm, Savannah saw Blake's love—and even more wonderful, his trust—written in bold strokes across his rugged face.

The breath she had been unaware of holding came out in a throaty laugh. "It's about time."

Linking her arms around his neck, Savannah drew Blake's lips down to hers and allowed herself to be persuaded.

Rebels & Rogues

All men are not created equal. Some are rough around the edges. Tough-minded but tenderhearted. Incredibly sexy. The tempting fulfillment of every woman's fantasy.

When it's time to fight for what they believe in, to win that special woman, our Rebels and Rogues are heroes at heart.

Cameron: He came on a mission from light-years away... then a flesh-and-blood female changed everything.

THE OUTSIDER by *Barbara Delinsky.*
Temptation #385, March 1992.

Jake: He was a rebel with a cause... but a beautiful woman threatened it all.

THE WOLF by *Madeline Harper.*
Temptation #389, April 1992.

At Temptation, 1992 is the Year of Rebels and Rogues. Look for twelve exciting stories, one each month, about bold and courageous men.

Don't miss upcoming books by your favorite authors, including Candace Schuler, JoAnn Ross and Janice Kaiser.

AVAILABLE WHEREVER HARLEQUIN BOOKS ARE SOLD.

my VALENTINE 1992

Celebrate the most romantic day of the year with
MY VALENTINE 1992—a sexy new collection of four
romantic stories written by our famous Temptation
authors:

> GINA WILKINS
> KRISTINE ROLOFSON
> JOANN ROSS
> VICKI LEWIS THOMPSON

My Valentine 1992—an exquisite escape into a romantic
and sensuous world.

 Harlequin Books ®

VAL-92-R

Take 4 bestselling love stories FREE
Plus get a FREE surprise gift!